ALSO BY KATIE GRAYKOWSKI

Romance

THE LONE STARS

Perfect Summer http://amzn.to/2EUwn0u

Saving Grace http://amzn.to/2BRSeTy

Changing Lanes http://amzn.to/2Fy5mNt

The Debra Dilemma http://amzn.to/2CItdHd

Charming Coco http://amzn.to/2CJqRaZ

Sage Advice https://amzn.to/2Tqnxd7

THE MARILYNS

Place Your Betts http://amzn.to/2BQYtqx

Getting Lucky http://amzn.to/2BSwk2v

Sorry Charlie http://amzn.to/2Fa0r7K

TEXAS ROSE RANCH

Texas Rose Forever http://amzn.to/2CLnMXS

Texas Rose Always http://amzn.to/2CMQ9oQ

Texas Rose Evermore http://amzn.to/2BS0eUk

Texas Rose Forgiven- https://amzn.to/2AyYL6z

THE FORT WORTH WRANGLERS

Lyric and Lingerie http://amzn.to/2BRYJFH

Harmony and High Heels http://amzn.to/2ETbdj7

The Tough Ladies

Cold As January https://amzn.to/2HxqXJS

Sweet Susie Sweet https://amzn.to/2JL8hTj

A Christmas Network Novel

Welcome To Christmas, Texas https://amzn.to/2B1yETJ

Mystery

PTO MURDER CLUB

Rest In Pieces http://amzn.to/2CJrxNz

Blown To Pieces http://amzn.to/2EVjm6U

Just One Piece http://amzn.to/2FxKiX9

Bits and Pieces https://amzn.to/37zY9sC

Urban Fantasy Sci-Fi

TIME, INC.

The Navigator -Out Soon

ABOUT RETURN TO CHRISTMAS, TEXAS

When veterinarian, Jules McCowan's best friend marries Santa Claus's oldest son, Jules has no idea that her life is about to change forever. It's been less than a year since she found out that Santa is real, reindeer can fly, and that Santa Claus traded in the snowy North Pole for the sunny, mostly snow-free Texas Hill Country.

Chris Van De Berg likes being Santa's second son. He's inherited all of Santa's charm with none of the responsibility. When St. Nicholas blessed his family with eternal life, he was also blessed Chris with the gift of compassion. He can look into a person's heart and feel what they feel … except for Jules McCowan. When he looks at her, all he sees is the person with whom he'd like to spend the rest of his life.

His Christmas wish has always been to find his soulmate.

Now that he has, how's he supposed to get Jules to fall in love with him? Around her all of the charm he's used to get people to do exactly what he wants is completely gone. In fact, he can barely get two coherent words out so how's he supposed to convince her that they belong together? Plus, if they do get married, she'll have to leave her life in the real world behind forever.

When Santa asks Jules and Chris to fly to France to check on Pere Noel's donkey, they leave immediately.

Chris has forty-eight hours outside of Christmas, Texas to persuade Jules that she's his destiny. If he doesn't return to Christmas, Texas within forty-eight hours, he'll never be able to return again and The Spirit of Christmas will die.

Will Jules take a chance on Chris and leave her life

behind? Or will Chris have to choose between her and The Spirit of Christmas?

RETURN TO CHRISTMAS, TEXAS

A CHRISTMAS NETWORK NOVEL

KATIE GRAYKOWSKI

For my grandfathers, Papa and Grandpa—I might not have been born into your family, but I got here as fast as I could. I miss you both and smile every time I think of you.

CHAPTER 1

Jules McCowan was covered from head to toe in animal muck. Not just dung and vomit and urine but mucus, blood, amniotic fluid, and something that looked suspiciously like pus, but without a microscope she couldn't be sure. All she was sure of at the moment was that she was exhausted and thankful she'd lost her sense of smell back in veterinary school.

"Doc, how much longer should this take?" Lucas Taylor wrung his hands like his wife, Shirleen, was in labor and not Apple Sauce, a two-year-old cow.

"Not too much longer, I hope." Apple Sauce was in a world of hurt. Her calf was breech, just as Apple Sauce had been when she was born. Breech calves could be genetic—at least that's what some research suggested. The "breech" gene came from the bull. It looked like Apple Sauce's baby daddy had the gene, just like her father had. Wasn't it just like a man to knock up a woman and make sure that birth was extra painful? And poor Apple Sauce didn't have the luxury of yelling at the father of her calf.

Life was so unfair.

"This calf is taking his sweet time coming into the world." Jules was almost shoulder deep inside Apple Sauce's back end. It was always a thrill, bringing a new life into the world.

Well, it was a thrill to bring animal babies into the world, not human babies. She'd been there for her godson's birth three months ago, and it was just plain gross. Her best friend, Lana, had given birth to a beautiful baby boy named Noel, but Jules could have happily lived without the front-row seat. So much fluid. She gagged.

Apple Sauce shot out a violent stream of diarrhea, which hit Jules directly in the face shield. Yep, still not as gross as human birth.

With one hand Jules held the calf's hind end, and with the other she grabbed one leg, bent the hock, and lifted upward, rotating it as she lifted. She drew the foot backward in an arc, keeping the hock joint tightly flexed as she lifted the foot over Apple Sauce's pelvis. She did the same with the calf's other leg. She waited until Apple Sauce had another contraction, grabbed both of the calf's hocks, and pulled. A beautiful baby bull calf slid out and landed on top of her.

He didn't cough, which wasn't a good sign, but he wasn't blue, so he had a fighting chance. The delivery had been long and painful for both mama and calf. Jules wasn't going to lose this precious baby.

She grabbed a piece of hay and rammed it up the calf's left nostril. He coughed out a wad of mucus, opened his eyes, and looked at Jules in stunned awe. It was so sweet.

Then again, cows always looked at the world around them in stunned awe; it didn't matter their age.

The calf rocked back and forth a couple of times and then stood on wobbly, unsure legs.

Apple Sauce began licking her calf clean.

"He's so beautiful." Lucas's gnarled, arthritic fingers wiped the tears from his hollow cheeks. He was eighty-two but didn't look a day over a hundred and forty. He felt around in his worn jean overalls. "Let me write you a check."

"I don't take checks, but I do take coconut cream pies." Jules slid her face shield and helmet off.

"No, I pay my own way." Lucas always put up a fight to pay with money she knew he didn't have. Being a small dairy farmer in a world of dairy-farming conglomerates meant that he barely made enough to squeak by.

She waved away the idea of money. "I have plenty of money, but I don't have a coconut cream pie."

That wasn't true ... well, the coconut cream pie part was true, but she also barely squeaked by. Being wealthy had never been her goal in life, which was good, because she specialized in large animals in a community full of small farms and ranches. As long as she could pay the mortgage on her office with its small attic apartment, she preferred to get paid in baked goods.

Last week, Lennar Pascally had paid her in cash for rehabbing his favorite mare, so she was flush for the next six months. For the next half a year, she'd be rolling in carbs.

Besides some sort of a love life, what more could a woman want?

She peeled off one of her full-arm disposable plastic gloves and tossed it in the trash can by the hose bib. She turned on the water with her ungloved clean hand and rinsed her face shield. She kicked off her work boots and rinsed them and then peeled off her other glove. Using the edge of the glove, she unzipped her brown coveralls, slipped them down, and stepped out of them. Underneath, she wore a Texas Aggies T-shirt and a pair of black leggings. Again using the edge of the glove, she spread the filthy coveralls flat on the ground and rinsed them thoroughly.

She looked down at herself. Water and muck had splashed up and polka-dotted her T-shirt and leggings.

Thank God she was on her way home after this, because it looked like she was competing in a Farmers Only wet T-shirt contest.

And she was pretty sure she smelled ... bad ... really bad.

"A coconut pie isn't enough." Lucas thought of himself as a mean negotiator. "Chocolate mint brownies too."

"Okay, fine ... but no more." She heaved a put-upon sigh like the brownies put the debt owed in her favor.

"You'll take a pie, brownies, and a rum cake." He folded his arms like the deal was final.

She stomped over like it was all way too much and he was twisting her arm. She held out her hand to shake on the deal. "Fine."

He shook it and stepped back like he'd just won the negotiations.

What the heck was she going to do with a cake, a pie, and some brownies? Her freezer was already full of other baked goods. It was time she bought another freezer. After all, when the zombie apocalypse came, she'd be trading cookies for gasoline and shampoo. Come to think of it, she could live without gas, but not shampoo.

The wind kicked up. It was early November in Marble Falls, Texas. Right now it was a humid seventy-five degrees, but an arctic cold front was on its way, so the seventy-five would drop to a cold twenty-nine by midnight. She liked cold weather. One day she was going to live somewhere it snowed, and not just an inch. She wanted enough snow to make snow angels and snowmen and snow forts. She'd learn how to sled and ski and ride a snowmobile. In her mind, there was always a roaring fire, hot chocolate, and a handsome man who looked a lot like Blake Shelton to come home to.

Lucas pulled out his phone and started filming the new calf. "I've got to get this on my YouTube channel."

Lucas had a YouTube channel? She made a mental note to look him up.

Jules rinsed everything again and then carried her better-looking but probably not better-smelling clothes to her truck and tossed her wet coveralls, boots, and helmet into the black plastic storage bin she had just to transport her yucky work clothes. She clapped the yellow lid onto the box and went back to the hose. She washed her hands thoroughly with antibacterial soap and turned off the hose. She'd forgotten to bring a towel to dry her hands, so she flapped them out in front of her to get the excess water off.

Dark pink, iridescent yellow, and purple colored the horizon as the sun yawned and stretched and finally slid down for the night.

Her stomach grumbled that it was empty, and she wished he had that coconut pie right now.

A pair of headlights bumped over the dirt road leading to the barn. It was Lucas's wife, Shirleen, in her old, blue Chevy truck.

"She's bringing you the pie, chocolate mint brownies, and the rum cake." Lucas's smile held a whole lot of yep-I-negotiated-exactly-what-I-wanted.

"You're pretty proud of yourself, aren't you?" She grinned at him.

"I was willing to add some pralines to the pot, but you settled too soon." Lucas laughed. "You should see your face right now."

"Dang it. I love Shirleen's pralines." Jules looked around at all of the pecan trees. "I thought the hail we had earlier in the year killed all of the pecans."

If Jesus came down from heaven and delivered pralines, they would taste just like Shirleen's.

"We had a few still produce. I cracked most of the pecans

myself." He nodded to the truck. "She has two dozen packed up for you."

Jules put her hand over her heart. "Thank God. I was seriously considering stuffing the calf back inside Apple Sauce just so I could get a payment renegotiation." She glanced at Apple Sauce, who was still cleaning her baby. "Sorry, I would have felt kinda bad, but I'd have done it."

At least she was honest.

Lucas laughed again and held out his hand for her to shake. "Thanks, Doc. You more than earned those pralines."

She shook his hand. "Apple Sauce did most of the work."

"Then why do you look so tired?" Shirleen called out the window of her truck.

The woman wasn't being rude, she was just being honest. Shirleen was a good, salt-of-the-earth Christian woman who didn't have time for BS, much less pleasantries, which was just one of the many reasons Jules loved her.

Shirleen opened the truck's door and stepped out. She walked around to the passenger's door and picked up a cardboard box. "The cake and the brownies are at the bottom and the pie is at the top. I packaged everything well, so you shouldn't have any problems."

She handed the box to Jules. It was heavy. Jules glanced down into it. By the waning light, she made out a pie tin, a square box, and a plastic rectangle, but the pralines were missing.

"And the pralines?" Jules no longer cared about the other desserts. She only had eyes for pralines.

Shirleen threw up a hand. "Oh, sorry. I left them on the seat. Let me get them."

She went back to the truck and picked up a paper sack. She placed it on top of the box.

"Thanks. I can't wait to dig in." Yep, she'd probably put away half a dozen on the way home.

Jules carefully placed the box on the front passenger's seat of her truck. She closed the door and walked back around to Shirleen and Lucas, who were talking about the calf.

"Thanks for all of the food." Jules waved.

"You're welcome. Thanks for saving the calf. Not many who would have had the skill to do that." Shirleen took a step back. "Normally, I would hug you, but I have to say you don't smell very nice. Go home and take a long, hot shower followed by an even longer, hotter bath, and then repeat."

Jules laughed. "I'm glad my sense of smell went bye-bye in vet school."

Shirleen breathed out of her mouth. "Do you need a trash bag to sit on to go home?"

"No, I have some seat covers." Jules waved again. "Call me if you need me."

She spread out a plastic seat cover and climbed behind the wheel of her truck. She was exhausted and looking forward to that long, hot bath.

She started the engine and leaned over the bench seat to grab her box of latex gloves. Yes, she'd washed with antibacterial soap, but still, she wasn't taking any chances. She slipped one hand into a glove, opened the paper sack, and pulled out a yummy-looking praline. She bit into it and almost swooned. She'd never thought of herself as a swooner, but here she was all holding back a swoon.

"I Want a Hippopotamus for Christmas"—her ringtone for her best friend, Lana—rang through the truck's speakers. The reason for the Christmas-themed ringtone when it wasn't even Thanksgiving yet was that Lana had married Santa Claus's son, Nick. At first Jules had thought about using "I Saw Mommy Kissing Santa Claus," but since Santa was actually Lana's father-in-law, it was weird.

Now that she knew Santa Claus was not only real but also a personal friend, she loved Christmas even more. Her vet office and the two-room attic apartment had been decorated for Christmas since before Halloween, but she drew the line at decorating the tree. Some lines even she couldn't cross—not because she didn't want to decorate her Christmas tree before Thanksgiving, but because she couldn't buy a real tree until after Turkey Day.

Jules hit answer on her truck's screen. "Hello."

"We have an emergency." Lana sounded stressed.

Jules's heart rate shot up to a bazillion beats per minute.

"Oh no, is there something wrong with the baby?" She might not have enjoyed watching her godson come into the world, but she adored him now.

"No, Noel's fine … I guess. Santa keeps stealing him. I have to kidnap my own child just to spend time with him." Lana laughed. "Santa loves kids … who knew?"

"Whew. I almost had a heart attack." Jules took another praline bite and chewed.

"The emergency is Prancer." Lana sounded worried, which just went to show that love really did conquer all, since before marrying Santa's son she'd hated Christmas. "She's sick. She won't eat."

Little-known fact, all of Santa's reindeer are female. Male reindeer shed their horns by the first week of December, while the females keep their horns through the winter. Since Santa's reindeer all have horns and vaginas, they're female.

"Okay." Jules glanced at the clock on her navigation screen. "I'm outside of Marble Falls right now. I can be there in thirty or so minutes. FYI, I spent all day delivering a calf, so I'm told I'm pretty smelly."

"Prancer won't care." Lana thought about it. "I don't think. But if it's a problem, you can shower here."

"Good. Can I also spend a good hour soaking in your enormous claw-foot tub? After Prancer, of course," Jules said around another bite of praline.

"A shower and a bath. Must be really bad." Lana laughed. "You sound tired, and what are you eating?"

"I am tired, and I'm eating one of Shirleen Taylor's famous pralines. If you're nice to me, I'll even share." She glanced over at the box sitting on the seat next to her. "Have a use for a rum cake and some chocolate mint brownies? I'm keeping the pralines and the coconut cream pie."

"What? I stopped listening after Shirleen Taylor's famous pralines. I can practically taste them now." Lana moaned.

"Can't you use the Spirit of Christmas to make her pralines?" The Spirit of Christmas was a million times better than Aladdin and his genie, because the Spirit of Christmas granted all wishes made in Christmas, Texas, no limit and no expiration date.

"Yes, but I really wish she'd give me her recipe. I've tried to make them and mine aren't quite right. Using the Spirit for a luxury and not a necessity feels all wrong." Leave it to Lana to put her own restrictions on wish granting. The woman loved to follow the rules.

Now Jules ... she hated rules. In her mind, she was a renegade ninja vet who could bust out some impressive ninja moves to save an animal from cruelty. Well, at least the vet part was true and the hating animal cruelty, but she doubted one semester of martial arts at Texas A&M qualified her as a ninja. But she was probably closer to becoming a ninja than Kylie Jenner, who hadn't had a semester of martial arts training that Jules knew of. Now that she thought about it, Kylie could afford to hire real ninjas, so why become one?

"I think the Spirit of Christmas likes being used. It's good to feel useful." And Jules liked to think that the Spirit of Christmas had a sense of humor, and unless Jules wished for outlandish things, like an actual space suit from NASA—FYI, the cloth is super itchy—how would the Spirit of Christmas ever get to laugh?

"What are the chances you asked for Shirleen's recipe?" Lana sounded so hopeful.

Did she not know Jules at all?

"Zero. I don't do recipes." Jules didn't cook. She was good at caring for animals; to be good at cooking too would throw off the balance of the universe.

"I guess that's for the best. The last time you tried using a recipe, the fire marshal came to your house and confiscated your grill."

"That wasn't my fault. If I didn't need an entire bag of charcoal, the bag should have said so. Nowhere on the charcoal bag did it say anything about a serving size. I'm sure lots of people stack an entire bag of charcoal into their tiny Webber personal grill and then stick the grate on top of Mount Charcoal. The fire was spectacular." She was pretty sure they could see it on the International Space Station.

"Okay, drive safe. I'll see you soon. I've got to go." Lana hung up.

The silver heart necklace that Jules wore around her neck warmed ever so slightly. Christmas, Texas, was hidden from the world, but Santa had given Jules a special necklace that let her see the town.

She touched it and felt a little zing run through her system. It was like the necklace was excited to be going home.

CHAPTER 2

Chris Van De Berg stood by Prancer's paddock and tried to look like he wasn't waiting for Jules. Being Santa's second son, he'd inherited all of his father's charm but none of the responsibility. Which was both good and bad. He was a hard worker and could smooth-talk anyone into doing pretty much whatever he wanted. That had always worked in his favor until he'd met Jules McCowan. Around her, he was lucky to get two words out of his mouth, and usually neither one of them made any sense.

But today was going to be different. He was going to finally charm Jules into having dinner with him. He put a hand to his queasy stomach. When he'd fantasized about finding the right woman and falling in love, nausea hadn't been part of the deal.

And yet here he was nauseated just the same. For this very reason, he'd skipped lunch. Nothing said "Have dinner with me" like tossing his cookies all over the woman he couldn't stop thinking about. Any way he looked at it, vomit wasn't romantic.

"Prancer." He scratched behind the reindeer's ears. "I

know you don't feel well, and I'm sorry I used your stomachache as a way to see Jules." He leaned in to the reindeer. "Actually, I'm really not sorry. This way I get to see her and you get examined. It's a win-win."

Prancer snorted and nuzzled him with her nose.

"At least you still think I'm charming." He rubbed the spot right above her nose.

She practically purred as she leaned in to him.

"You're flirty this evening." He went back to scratching behind her ears.

"I didn't know reindeer flirted," Jules said from behind him. "Is that part of their magical creature side?"

He dropped his hand and turned around. He could feel his face flushing red. It was dark outside and he wasn't standing in the glow of the exterior lights, so maybe she wouldn't notice.

"Do we need to have the you-can-love-your-animals-but-you-shouldn't-fall-in-love-with-your-animals talk? I'm not sure flirty falls under what's inappropriate or not." She laughed as she opened the paddock's gate, stepped inside, and closed the gate.

He just stood there and stared at her. His eyes went to her lips. He really wanted to kiss her, but they weren't there yet, and at this rate they never would be. After a few beats, her eyes narrowed. She looked like she was waiting for him to say or do something, but his brain seemed to have stopped working. She had really long eyelashes. He'd never noticed them before.

"That was a joke." She continued to watch him like she was still waiting for a reaction from him.

All he could do was stare at her. She was beautiful. Her chestnut hair was pulled up on top of her head in a messy ponytail. Her light-brown eyes always held just a little bit of mischief. Even in her splotched T-shirt and leggings, she was the most beautiful thing he'd ever seen.

Hadn't he just given himself a strong talking-to about not acting all weird around her?

"Tough crowd." She set her medical duffel bag on the ground and pulled out her stethoscope. "Okeydokey then. Down to business. Message received."

What message? When had he sent a message? What had it said? He looked around like a message would appear out of thin air.

She wrapped the stethoscope around her neck like she would use it later and scratched behind Prancer's ears. "Hello, my sweet girl, I hear you don't feel well."

Prancer leaned in to Jules.

"Would you mind if I examined you?" Jules ran her hand down the reindeer's neck.

Prancer stood stock-still like she was giving Jules permission to do whatever she wanted.

Jules plugged the ends of the stethoscope into her ears and grabbed the round disk. She ran it down Prancer's neck. "Lana said something about Prancer not eating."

He nodded his head furiously, but she was focused on Prancer, so she didn't see him. With all of his concentration he muttered, "Uh huh."

Check him out. He was able to utter a couple of groans that sounded like words. He wasn't sure that was progress, but he'd take it.

"Okay, lovely girl, your breathing sounds normal, unless flying reindeer breathe differently than regular deer. Then again, there's not a lot of creditable anatomical information about Santa's reindeer. The last article I read on them swore they ate nothing but sugar cookies and pooped glitter." Jules nodded to the paddock. "I see lots of poop and no glitter."

He stood there stone silent.

She shrugged and moved the disk down Prancer's neck. "I

don't see or hear any evidence of neck or throat trauma that would make swallowing difficult."

He grunted out another "Uh huh."

Sign him up for the debate team, he was on verbal fire.

"Okay, Prancer, I'm going to listen to your stomach to see if I hear anything out of the ordinary." Jules moved the disk down to the underside of the reindeer's stomach.

He liked that she was talking to Prancer and letting her know exactly what she was about to do. He was pretty sure Prancer understood English, or maybe it was just Jules's tone of voice. She had such a calming way about her … well, calming to everyone but him.

Jules squatted down as she moved the stethoscope disk around Prancer's undercarriage. "Um … uh oh. Huh?" She moved the disk around and looked like she was listening intently. "Oh no, that can't be right."

Something was really wrong with Prancer. His fear overrode his brain. "It's bad, isn't it."

He loved all animals, but Prancer was special. He loved her a little bit more than the other reindeer. She'd been born when he was ten years old, and he'd raised her as a calf back in the old country.

"Do you have any other reindeer here besides the ones that pull Santa's sleigh?" She looked around as if she expected to see some other reindeer.

"No … why?" What did other reindeer have to do with Prancer? Was it some sort of communicable disease?

She stroked Prancer's back. "Prancer's not sick, she's pregnant … with twins."

"What?" He held up a hand. "Wait, that can't be right. We don't have any male reindeer here."

"Crossbreeding with a whitetail deer is possible, but I don't think that's likely." She nodded toward Prancer. "She strikes me as a girl with high standards, so no average white-tail would do."

Prancer snorted her agreement.

"I hear ya. Finding a good man is tough." Jules patted Prancer's belly.

He wanted to raise his hand and tell her that he was a good man and he was easy to find since he couldn't leave Christmas, Texas. Was he a good man? He thought of himself as good, but wouldn't everyone think of themselves as good even if they weren't? More importantly, did she think he was a good man?

He was overthinking this.

He shook his head.

Jules slipped her stethoscope from around her neck and handed it to him. "You can hear the hearts beating."

As long as she stood there smiling up at him, he was prepared to do whatever she asked. He put the ends of the stethoscope into his ears.

Jules grabbed the disk end and placed it under Prancer's belly.

It sounded like a faint drum beating a fast rhythm.

She moved the disk over and there was another, slightly different, fast rhythm.

"Prancer's pregnant ... how?" He pulled the ends out of his ears.

"I guess I can explain the birds and the bees to you, but since you're an adult I would think it might have come up before now." Jules frowned. "Unless we're in a Forty-Year-Old Virgin situation, and then I have to confess I'm at a loss. Would you prefer I use the medical terms for body parts, or will the cruder street versions be okay?"

He waved it away. "No, I'm good with the sex part. My question has more to do with the access-to-a-male part."

The "male part" was a bad choice of words.

"Male part. That's funny." Jules laughed.

He blushed again. Thank God he wasn't standing in the light.

She patted Prancer's neck. "I'm willing to bet Prancer here went missing for a few days in late August or early September?"

"Yes, but she likes to roam ... ohhhh." He stroked Prancer's ears. "Looks like she had a better time on her vacation than she let on."

"I know. I kinda want to fist bump her, but she can't make a fist." Jules hip bumped her instead.

Prancer ducked her head like she was embarrassed.

He swallowed the gallon of spit that flooded his mouth. What was he supposed to do now? Should he go on talking about Prancer's sex life with Jules?

"Hey there, Julie." His father's voice came from behind him.

He always called her Julie or Julianna and not Jules. Chris just noticed that. When Jules wasn't in earshot, he really should ask his father why.

"Hey there, Santa." Jules hugged his father. "I like your new fashion accessory."

Chris turned around to find that his father was wearing baby Noel in a Babybjörn front-backpack thingy. His father was wearing his unofficial uniform of a Santa-themed Hawaiian shirt and board shorts. When he'd packed up and moved his entire Christmas operation here from the North Pole, he'd given up wearing pants except for Christmas Eve. Sometimes Chris had to wear sunglasses because the sun bouncing off those pasty-white knees was blinding.

"This baby-carrying thing is amazing. I can have my grandson with me and be hands free. True Christmas miracle right here." He pointed in the general direction of his grandson.

Noel started laughing and kicking his legs.

His giggly laugh was just about the sweetest thing Chris had ever heard.

Jules smiled. "He's laughing now?"

She touched the baby's fine blond hair, and he giggle-laughed some more.

"I know. It's the best sound ever." Santa patted his grandson's head. He turned to Prancer. "Twins? You really did have a much better time than you let on."

Chris had no idea if animals could blush, but he could swear that Prancer did.

His father glanced at him. "Hey, son, can you give Julianna and me a minute?"

"Sure." What could his dad have to say to Jules that he couldn't hear?

Chris slid his hands into his front jeans pockets and looked around for the best spot to eavesdrop without them knowing he was eavesdropping. He settled on her truck. If he stood on the other side of it, they'd have privacy but maybe he could catch a few words on the wind.

He walked around to the passenger's side of the truck and hoped the darkness hid the fact that he was watching them through the windows.

His father leaned in to Jules and said something.

Jules threw back her head and laughed.

It wasn't fair; he wanted to make her laugh like that.

Chris strained an ear, but he couldn't hear a thing.

His father nodded in Chris's direction, or maybe he was nodding at the truck—Chris couldn't be sure. He concentrated on his father's lips and tried his hand at lip-reading.

His father said, "Lightning booties in a roast," or maybe it was, "Biting noses at the coast," or it could have been, "Eating roses on some toast."

Chris knew he had many gifts, but clearly lip-reading wasn't one of them.

Jules leaned in to his father and said something. They both looked toward Chris, and then Jules's brow scrunched up and she shook her head. What was that about? Were they talking about him? He'd never thought of himself as the paranoid type, but they had to be talking about him. Or maybe her truck? But then why would he have to give them privacy?

Yep, they were talking about him.

What were the chances that his dad was really talking Chris up to impress Jules? The man was Santa Claus, so there was at least a chance that was the case; then again, he was also Chris's mischievous father who liked to play jokes on his sons. It could go either way.

His father waved him over.

Jules leaned down and kissed Noel on the cheek. He grabbed two handfuls of her hair and tried to put her face into his mouth.

"Oh no, he's trying to eat my nose." Jules laughed as she gently untangled her hair from the baby's hands.

"Son, I need your help." His father turned to him. "Père Noël's donkey can't stand. I need you to accompany Julianna to France so she may take a look at him."

So that's why they'd looked at him. He glanced at his father, who covertly winked at him.

Chris was pretty sure this wasn't a prank, but he'd been fooled before.

"I'm sorry Gui is sick." He was a tiny bit, but mainly he was excited to go anywhere with Jules, and he got to leave Christmas, Texas. It had been centuries. When his family had accepted St. Nicholas's offer to live forever, they'd also agreed to live with Santa Claus in the town of his choosing or the Spirit of Christmas would die. "How can I leave?"

"It's a special circumstance." His father grinned at Jules. "She's just agreed to be the official veterinarian of Christmas around the world."

Jules jumped up and down. "I'm so excited. I can't wait to see what other magical creatures I get to play with. Ahhh … so excited." She looked from him to his father and back at him. "Where are we going?"

"Pôle Nord. It's outside of Chamonix, France." Chris understood her excitement. Pôle Nord was one of his favorite places on earth. And he got to introduce her to it. "It's where Père Noël, or Papa Noel, lives."

Jules's brown eyes turned huge. "Is it cold there? Like snowing cold?" She clapped her hands together prayer-like. "Please say it is."

"Some of the best skiing in the world. Do you like to ski?" He couldn't help but smile. She liked cold weather too.

"I think so. I've never been skiing but it looks fun. Can you teach me?" She grinned up at him. "Please."

He wanted to give her the world. Now his mouth was bone-dry. Around her it was either feast or famine. He swallowed several times, trying to work up enough spit to speak. Finally, he was able to manage a word. "Yes."

Great, he was now back to monosyllabic words.

She threw her arms around him and hugged him tight. "Thank you."

He pulled her in to him and rested his chin on top of her head. He couldn't help but notice that she smelled bad … really bad. There was something dried in her hair. It smelled like … but it couldn't be … it smelled like dung. He sniffed again and his eyes started to water and then he started coughing.

She let go of him and stepped back. "I guess I need a shower. I was on my way home from delivering a calf when Lana called me."

She was embarrassed.

Santa snapped his fingers and the dirt and muck all over Jules disappeared. "The Spirit of Christmas comes in handy when you don't have time for a shower."

Chris should have done that for her. He hated that he hadn't thought of it.

"The Spirit of Christmas can do that?" Jules looked down at her perfectly clean clothes. "That's awesome."

Chris grinned at the excitement on her face.

His father laughed out a ho-ho-ho.

"So, we're going to France to help ... what was his name?" Jules glanced at Chris for help.

"Père Noël." Chris was very proud of his quick and coherent answer.

"Right." Jules looked at his father. "Let me get this straight, you only deliver presents to North America ... that's your territory."

"That's right. I'm in charge of Christmas gifts for the United States, Canada, and Mexico. And I head up the Christmas Network, which is comprised of all the other versions of Santa Claus from around the world. Every country has their own Christmas legends and traditions. Whatever version of a gift bringer they have is who covers their territory. Like Père Noël covers France. Sinterklaas covers the Netherlands. Father Christmas handles Britain."

"That's very smart. Divide and conquer." She nodded and glanced at Chris. "When do we leave?" She waggled her eyebrows. "Can we take the sleigh?"

That wasn't the exact moment he fell in love with her, but it was the moment he realized that he'd fallen in love with her.

CHAPTER 3

Nervous excitement jangled through Jules. Not only was she going to France, but she was going with Chris, who was cute in his charmingly uncharming way. Santa had whispered something in her ear about him, but she couldn't remember what it was. She searched her memory. It had only been a few minutes ago, but she couldn't recall whatever he'd said. She hated when her mind failed her. She searched her memory for important facts, like the anatomy of various animals, the names of all of the actors who'd ever played Doctor Who, and all of the current Real Housewives of Dallas. Check and check and check.

Cool, so she wasn't suffering from early onset Alzheimer's.

She turned to Santa. "What about the sleigh? Can we take it?"

It felt like she was sixteen again and asking to borrow her foster-mother's car.

Maybe what he'd said wasn't about Chris, but about the sleigh?

"You bet. Next to a wormhole that would get you to

France instantaneously, it's the fastest way to travel." Santa slid a hand into his left front pocket and pulled out a key ring with a huge silver skeleton key that had a cheery red glow. It wasn't an ordinary key; then again, Santa's sleigh wasn't an ordinary vehicle.

"Did you say wormhole?" Jules's excitement doubled, which was weird because she was already at a thousand percent. "Can the Spirit of Christmas create a wormhole?"

Santa laced his fingers on Noel's stomach and thought about it. "I don't know. I don't see why not, but testing it could punch a hole in the universe that could possibly kill everything and everyone ... or ... it could be a hoot to watch space and time bend." Using his hands, he weighed the good with the bad. "Possible universe-exploding event versus a good time playing with science. Probably shouldn't try it."

"Yeah, I agree." But traveling through a wormhole would have been nice. Speaking of wormholes ... "What's on Neil deGrasse Tyson's Christmas list?" She snapped her fingers. "Based on his past Christmas tweets, I'm guessing he doesn't have a Christmas list."

Santa shook his head. "Just because he values science above all else doesn't mean he doesn't have a Christmas list." He laughed and his whole belly shook. "I seem to remember bringing him a snow-cone maker last year."

Jules nodded. "I can see him as a snow-cone man. I bet he likes cherry."

"No, he's a coconut fan like me." Chris looked stunned that words were coming out of his mouth.

Jules nodded. "Interesting. I would not have taken him for a coconut man, or you for that matter." She took a step back and looked Chris up and down. "You just say grape to me."

Chris looked around nervously like he wasn't sure what he was supposed to say.

Awkward silence pulled out a chair and sat for awhile.

"You'd be surprised by what's on some people's Christmas lists." Santa put one arm around Jules and the other around Chris. "Why don't you tell her about some of the really funny items while in the sleigh on the way to France."

"Awesome. I'm going to ride in Santa's sleigh and get Christmas list insider information." Jules threw her arms up like her team had just won the Super Bowl. "This is the best Friday of my life."

"Not the best day of your life? Only the best Friday ..." It looked like Chris was back to talking.

"Yes, I've had some amazing Tuesdays and unbelievable Saturdays, but this is by far the best Friday of my life." She couldn't wait to see Santa's sleigh.

Santa snapped his fingers and they were in an open field standing in front of a huge red sleigh.

"OMG, we can snappy fingers from one place to another?" Jules snapped her fingers and she was sitting in the bench front seat of the sleigh. "It works. I may never walk anywhere again."

She snapped her fingers again and she was standing next to Chris.

"It only works in Christmas, Texas." Santa smiled down at her. It looked like he genuinely enjoyed the fact that she was having such a wonderful time.

Was this what it was like to have a father?

On impulse, which was definitely Jules's trademark reaction to everything, she stood on her tippy-toes and hugged Santa again. "Am I too old for you to adopt me? I want you and Nell as my parents."

She hadn't meant to say that out loud. She didn't tell people that she'd been a foster kid until she'd aged out of the system. Lana and Lana's mother knew, but that was it. Once people found out that she was a foster kid, it was all pity all the time.

Santa held her tight. "We're already your family. No adoption needed. I've watched you grow up." He loosened his grip and leaned back so he could look her straight in the eye. "Sorry I couldn't always give you everything on your Christmas list, but giving someone bubonic plague is against the rules." Santa winked. "Just so you know, Andy Cuzani still lives with his mother and makes rain ponchos out of duct tape that he sells on Etsy."

"I didn't know that duct tape is waterproof." She could see water-resistant.

"It's not, which is why he still lives with his mother." Santa continued to hold her loosely.

Baby Noel let out a cry of protest at being squished.

Jules stepped back and kissed the top of Noel's head. "Sorry I smooshed you."

"Who's Andy Cruising?" Chris looked from Jules to his dad and back to Jules.

"Andy Cuzani was my first love. He dumped me the day of the holiday dance so he could take Lisa Turner." Jules couldn't help the eye roll.

"Why would he dump you?" Chris made that sound like the dumbest thing in the world. "You're amazing."

He seemed truly dumbfounded.

"Thank you for that." She nodded toward Santa. "Sounds like I dodged a bullet."

Santa laughed as he handed the sleigh keys to Chris without looking away from Jules. "I want you to know that I respect women drivers. I'm having him drive you not because I don't think you can drive a sleigh but because only immediate members of my family can drive it. The Spirit of Christmas runs through our family."

Jules clapped a hand on Chris's shoulder. "The Force is strong with this one."

Chris glanced at Jules for explanation.

Santa's belly shook with laughter, which made Noel laugh. "He's never seen *Star Wars*."

Jules's jaw practically bounced off the ground. "Wow. I didn't know there were people in the world who hadn't seen *Star Wars*."

"Oh, right. That's a movie, isn't it?" Chris looked from her to his father and back to her.

Jules just shook her head. "I really don't know what to say to that."

"Forgive him. He's not as cool as I am." Santa shook his head too.

Chris held up a hand like a traffic cop. "Wait, I think I might have tried to watch it once, but I fell asleep."

"Fell asleep?" Jules looked up at Chris. "I don't think we can be friends anymore."

"Now hold on. That's a little harsh, don't you think?" Chris grinned down at her. "We should watch it together so you can wake me up in case I nod off."

Everyone she'd met in Christmas, Texas, always said Chris was a charmer, but this was the first time she'd sort of seen it up close and personal. "That's the most you've said to me since Lana's wedding."

Chris's eyes went huge, and she could swear he was blushing. "Um … I …"

It looked like he was back to speaking in grunts and moans. This was her fault. "Okay, stop talking my ear off and twisting my arm. I'll watch the entire series of movies with you, but I want movie theater popcorn, a Coke Icee, and permission to smack you if you talk during the movies."

He held out his hand. "Deal."

She shook it. "We'll watch them when we get back."

Chris glanced at his father. "How much time do we have?"

"You have forty-eight hours." Santa tickled Noel's tummy, which made the baby giggle and kick his feet.

Hands down, his baby giggles were the best sound she'd ever heard.

"I don't understand. What happens in forty-eight hours?" Did Père Noël need his donkey in two days?

What if the illness was something serious? She wasn't sure forty-eight hours would be enough for the animal to heal. Wait, Christmas wasn't until next month. Was French Christmas on a different day?

Leave it to France to be difficult.

"It's part of the deal we made with St. Nicholas. The Van De Berg family has to stay together in the same town or the Spirit of Christmas will die. I've gotten special dispensation for this trip, but except for Christmas Eve and the very infrequent work trip, we can't leave Christmas, Texas."

Jules went up on her tippy-toes and hugged Chris again. "I'm so sorry. How long has it been since you've left the town?"

"1820. That was the year we moved here from the North Pole." His eyes became distant like he was remembering something he'd enjoyed.

"Wow, that was a long time ago. So many things have changed. Don't worry, I'll catch you up ... women can vote, they've found evidence of water on Mars, and it has been proven definitively that the 'secret sauce' on the Big Mac is really Thousand Island Dressing." Surely he knew about the outside world. He was wearing jeans and a gray sweater. His clothes didn't look like they were two hundred years old.

"We have TV, movies, and the internet." Chris smiled. "I do try to keep current."

"Here I was about to give you a pass for not having seen *Star Wars* since you haven't left this place in a long time, and then you just dig that hole a little bit deeper." Jules washed her hands of him.

"Now wait a minute. Don't write me off. I'm still salvageable." Chris smiled.

It seemed that he was warming to her.

Jules hunched her shoulders. "Let's start with a *Star Wars* marathon and then we'll have to see." She looked directly into his blue eyes. "What's your favorite movie? It better not have subtitles."

"*Black Panther*." He didn't even hesitate.

She nodded. "I can work with that."

"You two have fun." Santa snapped his fingers and disappeared.

"Wait," she called after him. "What's wrong with the donkey?" Here she could snappy-finger whatever she needed to treat the animal, but what would happen there? "I don't know what medical supplies I should bring."

"Don't worry about it. Once we get there, the Christmas Spirit will supply what you need." Chris raised his arm like he was going to put it around her shoulders and then hesitated and dropped it.

Things turned awkward.

Jules snapped her fingers and the box of baked goods from her truck appeared in the back of the sleigh.

Chris pointed to the box. "You really don't need to bring supplies."

"Those are snacks for the road trip." She thought about it for a second. "Sleigh trip. I'm hungry, and if you don't count the pralines I ate on the way here—the exact number which I won't disclose—I haven't eaten since I had breakfast at five this morning."

Her stomach punctuated that last comment with a rumble.

Chris put his hand in the small of her back and led her to the passenger's side of the sleigh. He opened the door for her and then offered her his hand to help her climb up.

"Thank you, kind sir." She laughed. His manners were straight out of *Pride and Prejudice.*

"You must be starving." He closed her door and walked around to the driver's side. He climbed up and snapped his fingers. A white, rectangular, butcher-paper-wrapped bundle appeared. He handed it to her. "It's a gourmet Italian sub from a place called Tucci's in Austin. It's my favorite."

She unwrapped one end and took a huge bite. It had all kinds of meats and peppers and all sorts of veggies on fresh-baked French bread. It was fantastic.

"Don't you want to know what's in it?" He shoved the huge key into the small hole to the left of what looked like a cross between a car's steering wheel and that controller thing used to pilot planes.

"It's so good. I don't care what's on it. Hands down, this is the best sandwich I've ever had." She took another huge bite, chewed, swallowed. She held it out to him. "Want some?"

He glanced at the sandwich and licked his lips. "No, I'd better not. You should eat it. You haven't eaten all day."

She held the sandwich up to him. "Eat. There's plenty for both of us." She nodded to the box in back. "We can split the sandwich and the coconut pie."

"Did you say coconut pie?" He hit a button and a compartment behind the back seat opened and something slowly unfurled. It was a convertible top. It unfolded and covered the top of the sleigh.

"Yes, I did say coconut pie. If you play your cards right, I might even throw in some pralines, but I can't make any promises." Jules held the half-sandwich out to him.

He took a bite. He chewed and chewed and chewed. Finally, he swallowed.

She pointed to the roof. "I like the convertible top."

He shrugged. "It's cold outside and it's easier to drive without the wind practically blowing you into the back seat."

She took a bite of sandwich and then handed it to him.

He took a bite and then turned the key. There was a clicking noise and what sounded like an engine started.

She looked out the front window. "You're going to break my heart and tell me that the sleigh isn't really pulled by eight flying reindeer, aren't you?"

"Well, it is and it isn't. For short trips like this, we don't need the reindeer." He glanced down at her. "We can take them if you want."

She put a hand on his arm. "No, that's okay. I am glad to know that they really do help fly the sleigh."

"Are you ready?" Chris smiled down at her.

"I was born ready." She bounced up and down in her seat. "I can't wait."

Chris pulled the steering controller back, and the sleigh glided into the air.

Jules looked out the front windshield at all of the stars. "This is amazing."

They slowly made their way higher and higher. Jules stuck her hand out the passenger's-side window like a kid with the car window rolled down. This was almost as exciting as graduating from vet school.

"This is so much fun." She took another bite of sandwich and then offered it to him.

"I'm glad you like it." He took a bite.

They finished the sandwich, and Jules wadded up the butcher paper and leaned over the seat and stuffed it in the goodie box.

Was it her imagination or was Chris checking out her backside? She dismissed it and sat back down.

"Thanks for taking me." She bounced up and down again. "I can't believe I'm riding in Santa's sleigh."

Chris laughed at her enthusiasm. "Are you always like this?"

"Like what?" If he was giving her one of those back-handed compliments, she was totally going to rescind the praline offer.

"So excited by new experiences." Chris smiled down at her.

"I guess I'm a new-experience junky. I love to try new things. My mother died when I was a baby, and I have no idea who my father is. I grew up in the foster care system." She clamped a hand over her mouth to keep more words from spilling out.

She waited for the I'm-so-sorrys to swirl in the air. Instead, Chris just waited for her to finish.

"I didn't have a lot of new, exciting experiences growing up, so I guess I enjoy them now that I'm an adult." She took a deep breath and let it out slowly. "When you're a foster kid, you have very little control over your life. Someone tells you where to live and even what you can take with you when you move to your next foster placement. Everything was chosen for me. Now I get to choose where I go and what I do. I guess I collect new experiences like other people collect shoes because I can. I want to see and do it all."

She liked that he didn't press her for info, he just listened. And there was no pity. In her book, pity was right up there with a root canal on the list of things to avoid.

She yawned, and it felt like her long day was finally catching up to her. Her eyes were heavy, and she leaned against Chris's shoulder. His arm came around her, and she snuggled in even closer. He smelled like cinnamon and ginger.

She loved that smell.

The swaying of the sleigh was hypnotic, and Chris's shoulder was warm. She drifted off to sleep.

CHAPTER 4

Chris kissed the top of Jules's head as she slept with it on his shoulder. Hands down, this was the best sleigh ride he'd ever taken. He smiled to himself. In fact, this was the best Friday he'd ever had too.

Jules's body fit nicely against his. He wanted to drink her in and memorize every detail. He sniffed her hair. It smelled like lemons, which was a huge improvement, but if being with her meant he had to put up with dung, he'd take it.

Would it always be like this? In a couple hundred years would he still get flustered around her? He hoped so. She kept him on his toes.

That is, if he actually worked up the courage to make his move and they were still together in a couple hundred years.

He kissed the top of her head again. He could happily spend the rest of his life just like this.

Jules had mentioned being a foster kid twice, and he could feel how lonely and helpless and unwanted she'd felt growing up. He wanted to reach inside her heart and take that pain away, but St. Nicholas had only given him the gift of compassion, so while he could feel what she felt, he couldn't take that burden from her.

She snuggled closer into him.

Forget it being his best Friday, this was his best day ever.

She twitched and whimpered.

He could feel the sadness coming off her in waves. She was dreaming, and it wasn't pleasant.

He put the sleigh on autopilot and closed his eyes. He concentrated on her. He might not be able to take her pain, but maybe he could redirect her to a happier time.

In her mind he saw her as a nine-year-old girl with unruly brown hair and huge, intelligent, brown eyes. She was packing a duffel bag, and sorrow and fear saturated her soul. She was being moved to a different foster home.

"I'll be so good. I can help out with the baby. I promise. I'll be so good." Tears rolled down Jules's cheeks. "Please let me stay."

She was terrified. She wanted to stay more than anything.

Her foster parents were about to have a baby, and they didn't have enough room for her, another foster kid, and the baby.

Jules swiped at her tears. "I can sleep on the sofa. You won't know I'm here ... please." The desperation in her voice was hard to hear.

"I'm sorry, Julie, but we just can't. There isn't enough room here for you." The blonde woman was very pregnant. "Unfortunately, we only have room for one foster child. Charles has been here longer." She put a hand over her huge belly. "And this is a girl."

How could anyone not want Jules? He wanted to find this woman and ... do something really awful to her.

"Please ... I'll do anything." Jules hugged a pink bunny tightly to her chest. "Please let me stay. You won't even know I'm here."

"We just can't." The blonde was getting annoyed by what she thought of as Julie's over-the-top drama. "The social worker's in the living room."

The woman turned to head out the doorway.

Jules grabbed her hand. "I can sleep in the garage. I'll clean the house. I don't eat much. Please let me stay."

She was terrified of moving to another foster home.

He wanted to tackle her in a bear hug and tell her that everything was going to be okay.

The woman wrenched out of Jules's hold. "You have five minutes to finish packing."

This woman had zero compassion, and he could feel that she really didn't like kids, but her husband did, so she was resigned to having them. She walked out of the room.

And just like that, Jules was … thrown away … unwanted … alone … again.

He could feel her heart actually shatter.

Jules dried her tears, tossed her tattered pink bunny in the trash, and gave up on ever wanting a family. She promised herself that she would never cry again, because the only person she could rely on was herself. In that moment, she went from being a nine-year-old to being a jaded adult in the body of a nine-year-old. She stopped being Julie or Julianna and became Jules.

Not until she met Lana a little over a decade later would she finally feel some sense of belonging. His love for his sister-in-law quadrupled.

His heart broke for Jules. He'd never hurt so badly in his very long life.

Tears burned his eyes and he tried to hug her, but he was only a bystander in this dream. Since he couldn't physically comfort her, he tried to push love and comfort into her. She turned and looked right at him like she could see him in her dream.

His eyes slammed open. Had she seen him? How had she known he was there?

She slept calmly now, so maybe it had worked.

He hugged Jules even tighter. She'd been so small and felt so helpless. He wanted to spend the rest of his life making sure she never felt that way again.

She stirred and yawned. She opened her eyes and looked around like she wasn't sure where she was. It took her a couple of beats to realize she was cuddled into him.

"Oh my God. I'm so sorry. I fell asleep on your shoulder." She untangled herself from him and then touched his right shoulder. "Is that drool?"

Using the hem of her T-shirt, she tried to dry the damp spot on his gray sweater, but it was impossible.

He snapped his fingers and the spot dried.

"Hey, I thought we couldn't snappy-fingers things when we're away from Christmas, Texas." She reached into the back seat and rummaged through the box of snacks.

Chris had new admiration for the little girl who'd become this fantastic woman. "No, you can't … wait, what did you call it?"

"Snappy-fingers. I call it snappy-fingers when you can make something appear out of thin air." She turned back around and handed him a small, roundish cookie-like thing.

"What's this?" He sniffed it. It smelled sweet.

"It's a praline. Try it." She held up a finger. "Be prepared. You're going to fall in love … they're just that good."

He was already in love, and pralines had nothing to do with it. He took a bite. It was buttery and pecan-y and sweet. "It's good."

"Well that was lackluster. Try it again, but this time with feeling." She ate the rest of her praline.

"Okay, they're fantastic." He made sure his voice was extra excited.

"That's better, but it was still lame." She reached behind her and grabbed another one. "I'm not wasting them on you if you're not absolutely in love with them."

"I like them, but they're not Oreos." He was just being honest.

"That's not fair. Oreos are in a class by themselves." She pointed in his general direction. "Don't you dare snappy-fingers some Oreos and milk, because I'll be forced to reject the pralines and choose the Oreos. Since the pralines already have low self-esteem because you pulled the Oreo card, it could start a junk food war that would devastate the world as we know it."

"Who knew Oreos wielded so much power?" He loved the way her mind worked.

"They reign with an iron grip." She looked around like she was looking for an Oreo spy. "Total dictator situation. Junk food politics are complicated, and that's just the sweet side of things. When you add in the salty, it gets downright nasty."

She laughed. It was the best sound in the world.

He loved that she still saw the world as amusing. Had he been through half of what she had, he wasn't sure he'd still look at things and laugh.

She turned in her seat so that her back was against the passenger door and looked at him. "I want to know about the weird Christmas lists. Tell me everything."

He smiled. "Guess what Ringo Starr wanted for Christmas in 1969?"

"Less Yoko Ono?" She leaned forward like she couldn't wait to find out.

"Good answer, and probably by then he'd had enough of her, but no. His Christmas list that year involved an Easy-Bake Oven." Chris nodded.

"No." She thought about it and then nodded. "Maybe he

wanted to stuff Yoko in the Easy-Bake Oven?"

He nodded too. "I hadn't thought of that."

"How about I give you a name and you tell me what their weirdest Christmas list item is or was." She clapped her hands.

"Okay." He loved that she got so excited over the smallest things. She really did love and appreciate every new experience.

"Queen Elizabeth," she fired off.

"Henry VIII's daughter or the one currently reigning over Great Britain?" As it so happened, he knew both of their lists.

She arched an eyebrow. "Both."

"Elizabeth I wanted to be young forever, and Elizabeth II wanted stand-up paddleboards. We delivered on the paddleboards, but the fountain-of-youth thing was out of our control. Instead, Elizabeth I got a bag of rubies and a basket of fresh peaches." He'd always wondered how the rubies and peaches had gone over.

"Rubies and peaches versus stand-up paddleboards." Jules weighed the two. "I'm going to have to go with peaches and stand-up paddleboards." She shook her head. "I have no use for rubies."

He could see that about her. She was both practical and outrageous. Rubies wouldn't be her style.

"Now, if you'd given Elizabeth I the paddleboards and Elizabeth II the rubies, that would have been fun." She tapped her right index finger against her pursed lips. "JFK."

"A ukulele." Even he'd been surprised by that one.

"Mother Teresa." She threw out the name like it would stump him.

"That's easy. Gardenia bath bombs." He shot her a sideways glance. "Give me a hard one."

She smiled. "Janice Dorcas Fortemberry."

He shot her a one-eyebrow-up glance. "The one that died in St. Louis circa 1852 or the one that lives in Jasper, Texas?"

"The dead one."

"A camel. She wanted to name him Harold." He held up his index finger. Just to show her how much he knew, he threw out, "Incidentally, she died that New Year's Eve."

Jules watched him. "How?"

"She was an itinerant opera singer who celebrated a little too hard and fell off the roof of the Grand Opera House. According to the *Saint Louis Weekly Union,* she had a history of falling off roofs, only this time, the Grand Opera House was five stories tall. Before, she'd only ever fallen off one-story buildings."

"You'd think she would have figured out gravity the first time she fell off a roof." Jules thought about it for a second. "If I routinely fell off of roofs, I'd stop going out onto roofs."

"Yeah, me too." It was his turn to smile. "How do you know about Janice Dorcas Fortemberry?"

"I just made up the name." She tilted her head to the left and appraised him. "You made all of that stuff up ... didn't you?"

"Maybe or maybe ... not." He grinned and said, "Please give me Janice Dorcas Fortemberry's date of birth, manner of death, and Christmas list for 1852?"

A speaker on the dash lit up, and his father's voice boomed, "Janice Dorcas Fortemberry was born in 1815 in Natchez, Mississippi, to Hiram and Dorcas Fortemberry. Janice Dorcas was the fifth daughter and tenth child of Hiram and Dorcas. For Christmas in 1852, Janice Dorcas wanted a camel, four bottles of whiskey, and a red ostrich-feather boa. The whiskey and feather boa were delivered on Christmas Eve 1852. She died due to injuries sustained in a fall from the roof of the Grand Opera House in St. Louis, Missouri, on December 31, 1852."

"Wait a minute, the Spirit of Christmas comes complete with Santa Siri? That's awesome." Jules leaned close to the speaker. "Dear Santa Siri, please give me all of the Christmas lists for Lester Bacon-Batch."

Santa said, "There is no listing for a Lester Bacon-Batch."

"Please give Camilla Snodmill's Christmas lists." Jules laughed.

"I show no listing for a Camilla Snodmill."

"That's a bummer. I think old Camilla would want a name change for Christmas." She looked up at him. "Maybe she already got the name change, so now the Spirit of Christmas can't find her?"

"Or maybe she doesn't exist because you made her up?" He laughed.

"I don't know what you're talking about. The Snodmills have a long and proud heritage. They were world-renowned clockmakers ... the rock stars of the clockmaking world. They came over to America from the old country because of an indiscretion that involved Camilla's twin sister, Ludmilla, and Czar Nicholas II's half-brother Helmut the Hunchback."

"Helmut the Hunchback ... he sounds friendly. Did he live in a bell tower?"

"Of course. All hunchbacks live in bell towers, it's international law." She sat back. "Now, you see, originally, they were the Snotmills, but in 1902, the Ellis Island intake person thought he was doing them a favor changing it to Snodmill." She shook her head and put her hand over her heart. "Maybe if he hadn't changed it, they would have lived ..." She just shook her head.

"Oh no, what happened to the Snodmills?" He couldn't wait to hear what had befallen the made-up family.

"As the Snodmills were unable to find work on account of no one had ever heard of the Snodmill clockmakers, they were forced to join the circus and become flaming tightrope artists. On a good day, balancing on a tightrope is hard enough, but when you add fire, it's downright deadly. But what finally took them down was the hot-air balloons. They were the first, and unfortunately the last, flaming tightrope artists to ever attempt walking on a burning rope between two hot-air balloons."

"Wow, did they burn to death or fall?" He loved the way she looked at the world.

"Both." She held up one index finger. "Theirs is a cautionary tale. Never rent hot-air balloons from Bernie Hindenburg's Cut-Rate Balloons. If you're going to rent hot-air balloons so that you can walk a flaming tightrope between them, you want to pay full price. Scrimp somewhere else, but you should always invest in a quality balloon filled with helium and not hydrogen."

He laughed until his eyes watered. He loved her. How could he not? She was amazing.

CHAPTER 5

Jules was having the time of her life. She was flying in Santa's sleigh and hearing all of the Christmas insider gossip. Yep, definitely one of her top five Fridays.

"So, tell me about Père Noël. Is there a Mrs. Père Noël?" It was interesting that most cultures had their own version of Santa.

He glanced over at her. "There isn't. Now that I think about it, I should have noticed Père Noël's lack of female companionship before now. I guess I didn't notice it because of Père Fouettard."

"Who's Père Fouettard?" She'd never heard of him. Then again, until a year ago, she'd thought Santa was just a myth.

"He's Père Noël's counterpart. He's the one who punishes bad children while Père Noël rewards good children." He grinned. "He's the balance."

"There is no light without dark. Nor dark without light. Through balance, there is the force." Jules mentally willed him to know the quote.

He looked behind him like she'd directed the quote to someone else.

"Really? Nothing? It's from *Star Wars*." They needed to sit down and watch the series ASAP.

"That's that movie you want me to watch … right?" He waggled his eyebrows.

He was messing with her.

She laughed. "At least you recognize the name of the series."

Wait, Père Fouettard?

"Doesn't *fouet* mean whip in French? So, Père Fouettard is Father Whipper?" Jules shook her head. "Wow, that has a whole new meaning in this post–*Fifty Shades* world."

"Yes, he's Father Whipper, only I don't think he still whips children anymore, but I wouldn't put it past him. I'm almost a hundred percent sure that he hates children … and adults … and fun no matter who is having it." Chris didn't sound like he cared too much for Père Fouettard. "Now he's more of a companion for Père Noël."

A companion who hated all people and fun. Jules was willing to bet he was lots of fun at the company Christmas party.

"Where did Père Noël find Mr. Whipper? It must suck to be threatened with a visit from Mr. Whipper when all you get in the US is some coal in your stocking if you're bad." It would suck to have grown up in France.

"There are several stories about how Père Fouettard came about. The most popular dates back to 1150 AD. It says that three boys got lost—in some versions they were three wealthy boys on their way to an expensive boarding school, and yet other versions tell of three hungry boys who were out late walking through the grain fields looking for any grain that wasn't harvested." He waved the discrepancy away. "Anyway, three boys went missing, and it was said that a butcher, or in some versions an innkeeper, kidnapped the boys, robbed them, slit their throats, chopped them up, and threw them into a barrel of salted pork, thinking that he would either eat them or sell them as pork."

Jules raised her hand. "So happy to have grown up in the United States. All I had to worry about was a little coal in my stocking. The French are hard-core."

"Yes, well, the legend goes on to say that St. Nicholas learned of the boys, went to the butcher or innkeeper's house, and resurrected the boys. All three of them climbed out of the barrel and walked out of the house. The butcher or innkeeper was so amazed that he repented and vowed to follow St. Nicholas, and in some versions, St. Nicholas's punishment for the murderer is that he must spend the rest of his eternal life whipping children that misbehave. Either way, Père Fouettard was born. Regardless of whether he was repentant or it was a punishment, he's still whipping French kids, which I'm pretty sure he enjoys." Chris snarled. He really didn't like him. "Père Fouettard is the bad cop to Père Noël's good cop."

"Balance is very important … I guess. Give me a lump of coal over dismemberment any old day." She still couldn't believe that France had a kid murderer following their Santa around. Was Père Noël also a possibly reformed kid serial killer? "Did you ever ask Père Fouettard if he was a butcher or an innkeeper who kidnapped and murdered those boys?"

It was a fair question. Chris wouldn't have to rely on the legend if he had the man standing in front of him.

"No. No one besides Père Noël speaks to Père Fouettard. He's not a very nice man, and he doesn't have the best personal hygiene. If you're lucky, you won't see him." Chris sounded like he'd rather eat glass than see Père Fouettard.

Time for a slight subject change. "How long have you known Père Noël?"

"All of my life. He's my father's youngest brother. His name was Septimus until he became Père Noël." It sounded like he was just talking about basic family history and not the lineage of Santa Claus.

"Septimus … doesn't that mean seventh in Latin?" She'd spent a good amount of time learning Latin in school.

"He's my father's seventh sibling." Chris relaxed back against the seat.

"So, your grandparents named him seventh? Were they Borg? Like Seven of Nine?" She'd always thought that Seven of Nine should have been able to choose her own name or gone back to her human name of Annika Hansen.

Confusion played across Chris's face. "What are Borg?"

"*Star Trek* franchise. The Borg are a race of cybernetic organisms that link to a hive mind. Seven of Nine was human, but the Borg added her to their collective, and then she sort of regained her human side and turned against the Borg. *Star Trek: Voyager*." How did he not know this?

Chris watched her like she'd started speaking Mandarin. "What's *Star Trek*?"

She honestly had no idea what to say.

He shook his head. "Is that a book? Over the years I've read all of the books that are required reading in schools all over the world."

She just closed her eyes, pinched the bridge of her nose, and shook her head. He was comparing *Star Trek* to crappy stories like *Beowulf* … there just might not be any hope for him. Had *Beowulf* been a TV series, no one would have renewed it for a second season or probably shot a pilot for it in the first place. "I want more *Beowulf*," said no one ever.

"Oh, wait. Are you talking about *Star Trek* the TV show? I saw it a couple of times. William Shatner wanted an Academy Award for Christmas. Yeah, those have to be won."

"Okay, you get points for knowing what was on William

Shatner's Christmas list, but we have lots of TV watching to do when we get home." It was strange for her to be the one who kept things on topic. "Any idea why your grandparents named your Uncle Seven in Latin?"

"Because he was the seventh child and they spoke Latin, or, well, a mix of Latin, Gaulish, and Etruscan, which was pretty common during the end of the Roman Empire." He acted like it should have been common knowledge.

Her jaw practically dropped to her knees. "I keep forgetting you're really old."

"Just who are you calling 'really old'? I'm sixteen hundred and eighteen. I'm the youngest member of my family." He tried to sound offended but couldn't pull it off.

She patted his arm. "And you don't look a day over sixteen hundred."

She'd known he was old, but she'd never really thought about how old, especially in terms of history. "I bet you've seen a lot. The rise and fall of empires, the industrial age, world wars, the space race, Hershey bars ..."

What must it have been like living that long?

He thought about it for a couple of beats. "I've lived a long time, but we were pretty insulated in the old country and then the North Pole and now in Christmas, Texas. We get news of the outside world, but we haven't lived among it in a very long time."

It sounded lonely. Living forever, but completely out of time.

"Please tell me you've had a Hershey bar." She didn't like to pity anyone, but never having had a Hershey bar was pity worthy.

"Of course. I may be old, but I'm not stupid. Chocolate is a food group." He snapped his fingers and an enormous Hershey bar appeared.

"Yep, that's the biggest chocolate bar I've ever seen." She

took it from him. It had to weigh at least ten pounds. "Do you want some now?"

"No, not right now." He winked at her. "Just trying to impress you."

Why was he trying to impress her? It should have made things awkward, but she liked the idea of him wanting to impress her.

"It worked." She set it on the back seat. "Okay, so back to your uncle. How did he become Père Noël?" It was surreal sitting next to someone who'd been alive during the Roman Empire. She loved history, so at some point she'd pick his brain about what it was like.

"Did Lana explain how my father became Santa Claus?" He turned to face her.

"No." Jules thought about it. "She didn't. All she said was that St. Nicholas made him Santa."

"Okay, so you know that Santa Claus is based on St. Nicholas, who was a bishop in the village of Myra—what is now Turkey—in the fourth century AD. His wealthy parents died when he was young and left him lots of money. He used to leave gifts of money and treats for the families in the village. He heard of a poor man with three daughters who lived in the region. The man couldn't afford dowries for his daughters, so their chances of marrying were pretty slim. The man was concerned that upon his death, his daughters would have to resort to prostitution in order to survive. Bishop Nicholas left three bags of gold—one for each daughter—so they would have a dowry and the father would know that his daughters would be taken care of after his death."

"Women can take care of themselves." The idea that any woman needed a man to survive was insulting. Jules could feel her blood pressure rising.

Chris held up a hand. "It was a different time. Women

were only valuable in terms of what they could bring to a marriage, either in money or land or livestock. Also, how many children they could bear. It's offensive now, but then it was just how it was. For the record, I've always valued women for who they are and so has my father. One of those dowry-less girls is my mother. My father married her for love and didn't care whether she came with a dowry or not. He only took the bag of gold Bishop Nicholas had given her father in order to continue to give as Nicholas had done. My father used some of the gold to buy tools so he could make toys to give away to the children in the village. After almost three decades of toy making and giving toys to children, Nicholas—who'd died and become a saint by then—appeared on a road outside of our village and bestowed upon us the Spirit of Christmas."

"Which made your father Sinterklaas, who would become Santa Claus hundreds of years later." Lana had told Jules that part.

"Yes … right. At first my father could handle delivering presents to all of the children of the world, but after decades it became too much for one man to do all on his own, so my father asked his brothers for help. Since they already helped with toy making, it wasn't hard for them to start helping with the delivery. My father and his six brothers divided the delivery of toys among themselves."

"And Père Noël was born, essentially." Jules nodded. It seemed so normal that his uncles worked in the family business, but since the family business was Christmas, it was anything but normal.

"Pretty much." Chris reached over the seat behind him and picked up a praline.

"You secretly like them, don't you?" She wasn't above ripping it out of his hand if he just sort of liked them.

"They aren't Oreos, but they're pretty good." He grinned as he bit into one. "Not bad."

"What happened to your father's other siblings?" She turned around and got her own praline.

"We've only scratched the surface of what Santa looks like around the world. There's Father Christmas in England, Father Frost and Snow Maiden in Russia, Tomte in Sweden, Julenissen in Norway, Christkind in Germany, Austria, and the Czech Republic, and Los Reyes Magos in Spain. But my two favorite Christmas personas aren't actually people at all. In Finland, they have Joulupukki, which is a Yule Goat who drives a sleigh of reindeer that don't fly and goes around asking if there are good children here and then hands out presents. Now, my all-time favorite is Tió de Nadal in the Catalonia region of Spain. Tió de Nadal is a log painted with a smiley face who poops presents." He barely got out the last two words for laughing.

"I'm sorry. Did you say 'poops presents'?" Surely not.

"Yes, he lives under the Christmas tree and children 'feed' him dried fruits and nuts in the days leading up to Christmas. They wrap him in a blanket to keep warm. Then on Christmas Eve, they beat him with sticks and sing graphic songs about his bodily functions. The next morning, the household wakes up to find that Tió de Nadal has pooped out a pile of presents." He held a hand up. "I swear it's true."

She shook her head. "I don't know what's worse, a cannibal butcher or a present-pooping log. Where do people come up with these things?" The only answer was that people were straight-up crazy. "Is Tió the Present Pooper part of the Christmas Network?"

The Christmas Network was the organization that linked all of the world's versions of Santa Claus together.

"Tió de Nadal isn't a real magical creature." He made it

sound like the idea of Tió de Nadal as a magical creature was straight-up crazy. "No, that's just for real magical creatures."

"Until recently, I would have thought 'real magical creatures' was an oxymoron." Her magical creature horizons had definitely been broadened.

CHAPTER 6

Chris could happily spend the rest of his life riding around in the sleigh with Jules. She was smart and funny and beautiful. It would kill him if he had to let her go, but even if he could manage to sweep her off her feet and have her fall in love with him, she had to choose to give up her life in the outside world to be with him. It was asking a lot.

He made a silent vow right then and there to send Père Fouettard to that terrible foster mother's house and let him teach her a lesson she would never forget. What good was a grouchy people hater if you couldn't point them in the direction of someone who was hateful. Sure, there might be some ethical and possibly Spirit of Christmas backlash, but surely St. Nicholas would understand. After all, he was the patron saint of children, along with sailors, merchants, archers, repentant thieves, prostitutes, brewers, pawnbrokers, and students. Now that he thought about it, St. Nicholas was probably too busy patron-sainting all of those people to notice Père Fouettard going on a special errand.

Jules covered her mouth as she yawned. "At the risk of sounding like a five-year-old, are we there yet?"

"Hey, don't knock five-year-olds. I like five-year-olds." Mentally he reviewed the last sentence. "That didn't come out right."

"That statement taken out of context could be construed as strange, but under the circumstances, I know what you mean. All I really wanted to know is if we're close." She yawned again and added a full-body stretch to punctuate her fatigue.

He looked down at the small screen above the flight controls. "Should land in about thirty minutes."

Jules thumbed in the direction of the back seat. "Mind if I take a quick nap in the back?"

"Go right ahead." He positioned his right arm along the seat back. "Or you could use my shoulder again. It's a better pillow than that Hershey bar."

Jules glanced in the back seat and then back at him. "I'm having a hard time deciding between comfort and the idea of a Hershey bar pillow. True, the Hershey bar won't be comfortable, but it's a pillow made of chocolate." She pointed to his shoulder. "What about the drool from earlier?"

She sounded only slightly embarrassed.

"What drool?" He would have put up with way worse things to have her in his arms. "I have no idea of what you speak."

"That's the right answer." She snuggled into him and placed her head on his shoulder. She was out in a matter of seconds.

He closed his eyes and concentrated on her and opened his mind. He pushed love and happiness into her. Her whole body sighed as she relaxed even further into sleep.

More than anything, he wanted to step into her dream, but her dreams should be her own. Yes, he'd interfered earlier, but he told himself that was okay because he'd sent her down a nicer, kinder dream path.

Forty-five minutes later, he hated to wake her, but they'd landed.

Gently, he tucked a lock of her hair behind her ear and then shook her shoulder.

She startled awake and sat up. She looked around like she wasn't quite sure where she was, and then recognition ironed out the wrinkles on her forehead.

"We're here." He pointed to the overly fussy red house. If a gingerbread house from hell and a Swiss chalet had a baby, this is exactly what it would look like.

"That is a whole lot of red against the white of the snow." She leaned in closer to the windshield. "Does it glow like that in the daytime?"

"Yes." He'd always thought it was the evil radiating off of Père Fouettard that powered the red glow.

A knock came from the driver's-side door.

Chris glanced out the window and cringed. Even Père Fouettard's knock was menacing.

"Time to meet Père Fouettard." He grimaced. "I was hoping for Père Noël."

"Not me. I like to get the bad news out of the way so I can enjoy the good news." Jules opened her door, a gust of frigid wind blew in, and she closed her door, shivering. "Can you snappy-fingers me something warmer, please?"

"I'm sorry. I should have thought of that." He shook his head at his thoughtlessness and snapped his fingers.

A butter-yellow snowsuit covered her from head to toe.

"I love the color. It's one of my favorites." She pulled on the gloves that appeared in her lap. "I can't wait to meet Father Whipper."

"I don't know why. He's not a very nice person." He was willing to admit that he might have been scared of Père

Fouettard when he was a child. And possibly some of that fear still lingered.

He snapped his fingers and a black snowsuit covered him.

Jules went to open her door.

Chris threw out a hand. "Wait. Let me come around to get you."

His mother would kill him if he didn't open doors for ladies. It might be old-fashioned, but he didn't care.

Jules opened her own door. "Too late."

She slid out of the sleigh.

Chris threw open his door, ignored Père Fouettard, who was glaring at him, and went around to help her anyway.

He grabbed her arm and whispered close to her ear, "Don't stare at Père Fouettard. It makes him even angrier than his normal sour disposition."

She leaned in to him. "How bad are we talking? I'll try not to stare, but until I see what we're working with, I can't make any promises."

They walked around the front of the sleigh.

Père Fouettard stepped in their way. "I told your father that we don't need any help with Gui."

"Holy cow." Jules glanced up at Chris. "Sorry, all bets are off."

She looked down at Père Fouettard and held out her hand for him to shake. "Has anyone ever told you that you look a lot like Lord Farquaad from *Shrek*?"

Père Fouettard looked at her hand and then up to Chris. "What is *Shrek*?"

"It's an animated film. One of my favorites." Chris studied Fouettard. Now that Jules had pointed it out, he did look like the diminutive Lord Farquaad.

"I love it too." Jules withdrew her hand.

They were finding more things in common every minute they spent together.

"Tell me about Gui." Jules didn't seem the least bit fazed by Fouettard's refusal to shake her hand.

"We don't need any help with her. She's fine. She's just tired." Père Fouettard clearly didn't want them here.

Jules put her hands on her hips. "When did you graduate from veterinary school? I'd like to see your diploma."

Père Fouettard growled at her.

Jules growled back.

They glared at each other in an epic stare-down battle.

Fouettard blinked first.

Jules was nothing short of amazing.

Fouettard pointed at Jules. "She is very rude."

"Rude … me? I don't think so." Jules's voice turned squeaky. "Pointing at me and talking about me like I'm not here is rude. I'm not the rude one. Did I ask if you'd murdered any kids lately and cut them up to make stew? No … because I have manners."

Fouettard growled again.

Jules looked down her nose at him. "Don't growl at me again. We both know I just won the staring contest. Now take me to Gui."

Fouettard growled again but motioned for them to follow him.

Jules had just tamed the only person in the world who he'd thought couldn't be tamed. He'd seen more than a few miracles in his day, but this just might top them all.

Fouettard slid the barn door open, and inside Gui lay on her side like a huge dog. She seemed to be panting like a dog.

Jules practically hurled Fouettard aside to get to Gui.

"Hello, beautiful girl." She dropped to her knees and stroked the white and gray donkey. "You look like you don't feel good. You're breathing very fast. Let's see if we can make you feel better."

She snapped her fingers and her stethoscope appeared.

She plugged the ends into her ears and used the flat, round disk to listen to Gui's belly.

Chris half expected her to tell Fouettard that Gui was pregnant.

Jules's face screwed up, and Chris could feel the worry coming off her in waves. Gui wasn't going to have a baby, she was really sick.

"When was the last time she ate?" Jules barked but didn't look up from Gui.

"Yesterday. She won't take any food or water today." Fouettard stomped over to Jules. He lorded over her … or, well, lorded as much as a man who was four feet tall could lord.

"When did she first start acting dull?" Jules unplugged the stethoscope from her ears and wrapped it around her neck, never taking her eyes off of the donkey.

"Dull?" Fouettard glanced at Chris for explanation.

Chris hunched his shoulders.

"Dull .. you know … sad … depressed … not her usual self." Jules ran her fingers down Gui's neck like she was feeling for something.

"I guess she's been depressed a couple of days." Fouettard squatted down. "What is it?"

"I don't know for sure yet." She ran her fingers up Gui's neck to her ear. "I need a blood swab."

She snapped her fingers. A pipet appeared. Gently she pressed the pipet to Gui's ear, and a drop of blood welled up. She snapped her fingers again and a small rectangle of glass appeared. She swiped the glass across the blood droplet, smearing it on the glass.

"You are very brave, my sweet girl. I know that had to hurt." Jules rubbed the spot where she'd drawn the blood.

Jules snapped her fingers and a flashlight appeared. She flicked on the flashlight and held the blood in front of it.

She shook her head. "Hyperlipemia. See the blue tinge to the blood? She has hyperlipemia."

"What is that?" Fouettard stared at Gui as if he would be able to see disease.

"It's an imbalance caused when fat reserves are sent to the liver to be converted to glucose for energy. That is a normal bodily function, but donkey physiology isn't good at turning that process off after enough glucose is created, so fat levels continue to increase, which can lead to kidney and liver degeneration and failure." Jules took a deep breath and let it out slowly. "Since she's obese, I'd say she also has an insulin-resistance issue."

"Can you heal her?" Fouettard's bravado crumbled.

Chris couldn't believe that the man he'd thought couldn't love loved this donkey.

"Yes and no. We can treat the underlying condition with painkillers, vitamins, and antibiotics. I'll start her on fluids right now to see if we can ease her pain and balance out the insulin and glucose in her system." Jules looked him square in the eye. "The prognosis for donkeys with hyperlipemia isn't good. She's obese, which doesn't work in her favor."

"Please help her." The naked pain on Fouettard's face was hard to watch.

Jules reached out and patted his arm. "I'm going to fight to save her. I don't know much about the anatomy of flying donkeys, but I'm going to do anything and everything to save her."

Fouettard sat on the ground next to Gui and put her head in his lap.

The thought that the man could love something should have made Chris happy, but it was creepy.

"I knew Julianna could help Gui," Père Noël said from behind Chris.

Chris turned around and was enveloped in a bear hug by his uncle.

"She's doing her best." Chris couldn't help feeling pride in Jules. He really didn't have a right to claim that pride, but he felt it anyway.

His uncle let him go and stepped back. "So tell me about Gui."

Jules stood and offered her hand. "I'm Jules, by the way."

Père Noël bypassed the hand and went in for a hug. "I know, Julianna. Santa's told me so much about you."

Jules laughed. "You're a hugger just like Santa."

Père Noël let her go and stepped back. "Can't help it. I come from a long line of huggers." He knelt next to Gui. "How is she?"

"She has hyperlipemia, which can be very painful. I was just about to start her on fluids." Jules snapped her fingers and an IV pole complete with a clear, liquid-filled bag appeared.

She snapped her fingers and a small tube with a needle on one end and an IV port on the other appeared. She felt around on Gui's neck. Using her teeth, she pulled the cap off of the needle and worked it into Gui's neck.

Gui didn't even flinch.

Jules screwed the IV bag's tube into the IV port, and liquid started running down the small tube and into Gui. Jules snapped, and a syringe appeared. She pulled the cap off the syringe and stuck it into a smaller IV port in the long tube that came from the bag.

Gui's breathing started to even out.

Jules stroked Gui's neck. "I know … I know … that takes some of the pain away."

Gui's ears twitched, and she started rocking back and forth like she wanted to get up.

Jules rolled out of the way while trying to hold the IV in

place. "We need to keep her as still as possible for the next few hours.

Père Noël turned to Chris. "Can you try to calm her down?"

Chris knelt beside Jules and laid a hand on Gui's neck. "Shhh … it's alright."

Sometimes he could use his special gift on animals.

He closed his eyes and concentrated on her. "Try to stay still. I know the pain is getting better, but you need to stay still."

He'd found that animals thought in pictures, and they felt love and dislike for the things they pictured. He sent Gui the image of an apple, and her whole body smiled. The picture of an almond croissant popped into her head, and he could practically taste the almond paste used in the croissants.

Chris laughed and opened his eyes. "Who's been feeding her almond croissants?"

Père Noël glared at Père Fouettard. "You told me you stopped feeding them to her."

"I only give them to her every once in a while." Fouettard wouldn't meet anyone's eye.

Jules was furious. Chris could feel the anger coming off her.

"How often? And how many do you feed her at a time?" Jules gritted her teeth.

"I've cut back. She only gets two or three ..." Fouettard had the good sense to sound chastised. "… a day."

"A day? *A day.* Are you serious?" Jules was fuming. "That's the reason she's so sick. Donkeys can't process that kind of carb load. Donkeys have a sweet tooth and should be given treats rarely. Those treats should be fruits and vegetables."

Fouettard stared at the floor. "But she likes almond croissants. She's French. We eat croissants." He sounded like he knew he'd screwed up.

"From now on, she gets only apples and carrots as treats. Surely she can still be French without the croissants." Jules sounded like she wanted to ram something really sharp into Père Fouettard's eye.

"Yes." Père Fouettard sounded contrite. "No more croissants."

Jules rolled her eyes and sighed like she'd had enough of stupid animal owners. Chris could feel her working to calm herself down.

She took a couple of deep breaths. "Donkeys are very intelligent and like a challenge. Try putting an apple in a bucket of water and make her bob for it. Or cut the apple into wedges and hide them in her straw or under a bucket or inside of a hollow log. Make her work for her treat."

Fouettard looked up. "I can do that. Gui's very smart. She would love searching for her treat."

And just like that, Jules tamed Father Whipper.

CHAPTER 7

Jules sat on the barn floor next to Gui and stroked her neck. She studied Chris.

She shook her head. "I don't understand. How did you calm Gui?"

Père Noël folded his long, lanky frame and sat next to Jules. "St. Nicholas gave Chris the gift of compassion when he bestowed the Christmas Spirit on him. His mother has the gift of time, his brother the gift of knowledge, his father the gift of seeing the true heart of a person, and Chris has the gift of compassion."

Jules nodded. That sounded well and good, but what did it have to do with animals? "How does that work on animals?"

"It doesn't work on all animals, but it works on some. I've found that animals think in pictures and feel emotions based on the pictures they see in their head. They also recall pictures sometimes based on smell. Words don't work, just pictures and scent. I calmed Gui down by sending her a picture of an apple. She loves apples, so she relaxed. Then she thought about a picture of an almond croissant. That's how I knew someone was feeding them to her." Chris turned to Père Fouettard. "Almond croissants are her most favorite thing."

Everyone looked at Père Fouettard.

He rolled his eyes. "I told you I wouldn't feed them to her anymore. What more do you people want?"

Jules made a V with her fingers and then pointed to Père Fouettard in the universal I'm-watching-you gesture. He better not give Gui even a bite of anything that wasn't approved by her.

She turned back to Chris. "I read a study where they did an MRI on a dog's brain for a baseline and then they rescanned him after he'd been given a piece of clothing worn by his owner. The pleasure centers of the dog's brain lit up just like a human's brain does when they see someone they love." She stroked Gui's muzzle. "Maybe it works like that."

"I don't know for sure." Chris closed his eyes and appeared to be concentrating. "Gui is feeling better, but she doesn't understand why she feels fuzzy. She loves all of the attention." Keeping his eyes closed he said, "Fouettard, put your hand right by her nose."

"Why?" Fouettard looked wary, like he half expected Chris to make Gui bite him.

"A little experiment. I want to see who is the most comforting to Gui." Chris looked like he was still concentrating on Gui.

Fouettard leaned over and gently scratched Gui's muzzle. He sat back and stroked her head.

Chris laughed. "Now, Père Noël, take your turn letting her smell you."

Père Noël squatted down and patted Gui's nose.

Chris's shoulders shook in laughter. "Now Jules. Let her smell you."

Jules was always game for an interesting experiment. She

scratched the gray velvet of Gui's nose and then went back to stroking Gui's neck.

Chris laughed. "She doesn't like you very much. She doesn't hate you, but she thinks you're mean."

Gui brayed like she was confirming the comment.

"That's not very nice. I'm not mean." Jules had never thought of herself as mean.

"Here, let me show you." Chris took her hand. "Close your eyes and concentrate on Gui."

Jules closed her eyes and tried to think only of Gui. She wasn't sure if she should think of the donkey as a whole or try to focus on the donkey's mind.

"Just picture her. That should be enough." Chris stroked the back of her hand with his thumb.

It felt good, but was she really feeling good or was this Gui?

Chris laughed. "That's all me."

He could read her mind? That was both awesome and rude. They were going to talk about mind-reading boundaries.

"I don't read minds, I read emotions." Chris sounded very pleased with himself.

"Then how did you know I was thinking about how rude it was for you to read my mind?" It was super hard to roll her eyes while they were closed, but she did it anyway.

"Just picture Gui." Chris sounded like he was really enjoying himself.

She pictured Gui. "Okay, got it."

"Uncle, let her sniff your hand again." Chris stroked the back of her hand again.

She concentrated on Gui and refused to acknowledge that it still felt good.

Jules felt her whole body relax. Gui pictured herself flying through the air with Père Noël on her back. Jules could feel the cold wind on her face as she—or, well, Gui—raced through the air. The donkey loved having a job, and she adored Père Noël.

"Now, Père Fouettard, you let her smell you." Chris continued to hold Jules's hand.

"This is stupid." Père Fouettard shuffled around, and Jules guessed he was moving so that he could let Gui sniff him.

Gui's whole body smiled. While she adored Père Noël, she loved Père Fouettard. He was her most favorite person in the whole wide world. She pictured him feeding her almond croissants and the two of them going for a walk. She liked to put her head on his shoulder. He would whisper to her. She didn't understand that he was using words, she just liked the tone of his voice.

"Now Jules. Let her sniff you," Chris said.

With her eyes closed, she drew her hand down Gui's neck until she felt her muzzle.

Gui's body cringed. She associated Jules with pain. The donkey fought the urge to get up and run away.

"That's not fair. I was only trying to help." Jules pulled her hand away.

"No, put your hand under her nose again. I'm going to try to explain that you aren't the reason for her pain and that you're here to help." Chris made it sound like that might just be impossible but he was going to try.

In her mind's eye, she could see Gui slowly getting up, feeling no pain, and running through a field of wildflowers with Jules leading her the whole way. Some of Gui's fear of Jules causing her more pain subsided. Gui put her head on Jules's shoulder as they walked in the same flower-covered field. Gui no longer felt wary of Jules. She didn't love or adore Jules, but she wasn't scared of her anymore.

Well, that was a start.

Jules opened her eyes and scratched behind the donkey's

ears. Gui's whole demeaner had changed to one of calm instead of stress. "That was amazing."

"I do have my moments." Chris smiled.

She could swear he was flirting, but then again, it had been a really long time since she'd flirted with anyone, so her flirt-o-meter might be broken.

"No, you're right, I'm flirting with you." Chris tried to pull off humble but didn't. There was too much confident male.

"We really need to talk about you reading my mind." She wasn't sure how she felt about the flirting, but she knew she hated not being able to think privately to herself.

"I can't mind-read, but I guess I can heart-read." He thought about it. "Yes, that has to be it. I've never been able to mind-read before."

Lucky her ... she was the first. "Whether it's mind-reading or heart-reading ... stop it. I don't like it."

He shot her an overly bright grin. "At least Gui isn't afraid of you anymore."

How did he know just how to get her? Animals had always been her soft spot.

She waited for him to comment on her internal dialogue, but he just smiled down at her. Maybe he had turned off whatever he used to read her heart.

Jules yawned and stretched.

"You must be tired. It's very late back in Texas." Père Noël stood. "Let me show you to your rooms."

"I can't. I need to stay with Gui." Jules yawned again. She was exhausted, but she had a patient who needed her.

Père Noël nodded toward Père Fouettard. "He won't leave her side. Tell him what to do."

Jules was about to argue, but her mind was getting fuzzy from lack of sleep. Maybe her being tired had been how Chris was able to read her mind. She glanced at Fouettard. "When that bag of fluids runs out, you need to replace it."

Fouettard snapped his fingers and the bag refilled. "I'll just keep it filled up. Do I need to give her another shot of medication?"

She should have thought of the refilling bag. It was so *Harry Potter*. Was J. K. Rowling really a witch? Since there were magical creatures, why couldn't Hogwarts be real?

"No, she won't need another shot for several hours. Just try to keep her down and calm. I'd love it if she got some sleep." They were in France. Would it be too much to ask to see Beauxbatons Academy of Magic? If she asked, would they think she was crazy? Where was Chris's heart-reading ability now?

Fouettard nodded. "I'll keep the bag refilling."

He looked as worried and exhausted as she. "You could use some sleep too."

He waved the idea away. "I'll be fine. I'm not leaving Gui even for a second."

She knew how he felt. Maybe she should stay here and watch over the donkey.

Chris reached over and took her hand. He practically pulled her up. "You need sleep. I'm not taking no for an answer."

He was right, and she knew it, but she hated to leave a sick animal. "I know, but …"

"But nothing. You're no good to Gui if you're exhausted." Père Noël put his arm around her shoulders. "You need to sleep. Gui's resting and so should you."

Chris put his arm around her waist. "Gui will be fine." He glanced back over his shoulder. "She's in good hands." He shook his head and whispered, "I can't believe I actually think Père Fouettard's hands are good."

"I heard that," Père Fouettard said from behind them.

"I don't care. Your past history doesn't exactly qualify you as nurturing." Chris didn't even look back at Fouettard.

"A man makes one little mistake and the world hates him forever." Fouettard sighed like he'd been unfairly accused. "Yes, I did kill those boys, but so what? They were stealing apples from my cellar. They were thieves. History doesn't seem to remember that."

"Stealing apples justifies murdering them?" Jules had almost forgotten that Fouettard was a very bad man.

"I caught them red-handed—"

"Which is a curious mental image considering you dismembered them so you could eat them." Jules couldn't believe she was actually having this conversation.

"That is a lie. I wasn't going to eat them. I was going to sell them as pork." Fouettard sounded like that was an important distinction.

"Oh, sure. That makes cannibalism okay. It's okay as long as you think it's pork. Yummm … human, it's the other white meat." Jules tried to remind herself that the man wasn't all bad. He loved Gui, which was something.

Fouettard glared at her and crossed his arms.

At least he had the common sense to shut up.

Père Noël dropped his arm, opened the barn door, and waited for them to walk outside.

They stepped into the snow. It was about ankle deep and crunched under her snow boots. It looked like someone had painted the entire world white, or, well, metallic gray as the full moon glowed on the glittering snow. It was peaceful but also unsettlingly silent. Silence had always made her uncomfortable. Growing up in foster homes and then a group home, there was never silence. She'd always thought she wanted it, even craved it in high school, but when she moved out on her own after college, the silence had been unbelievably loud.

A shudder ran through her.

"Are you cold?" Chris slid his hand up her back and put

his arm around her shoulders, trying to shelter her from the wind.

There was something safe about being around him that was both comforting and scary. She was the only person whom she trusted to provide her safety. She didn't need a man or anyone for that matter to make her feel safe. She was perfectly able to do it all on her own. Grudgingly she admitted that it was nice to have someone make her feel safe.

"That looked hard and slightly painful," Chris whispered close to her ear.

"What?" Was she hearting-thinking again? She really needed to figure out how to close off her mind or heart so he couldn't read it.

"Whatever realization you just came to. You looked like you were trying to remember pi to the millionth place." Chris's voice tickled her ear.

Jules blew her bangs out of her face. "I was just admitting something to myself that I really didn't want to admit."

"I hate it when personal growth happens. I prefer being shallow and completely clueless." He laughed.

"Oh my God, you're one of those people who watches movies for the character development." She laughed too. He was anything but shallow.

"Nope, I just want to watch stuff blow up." He was all honesty.

"I don't believe that for one minute." She cut her eyes to the left and analyzed him. "You strike me as a foreign art film kind of guy. Otherwise, you'd get my *Star Wars* references."

"Don't box me in. I'm a man of varied tastes. I like a good car chase as much as the next man." Chris gently led her to the red-glowing house.

"Don't believe him for a minute. The outer shell is shallow, but deep inside beats the heart of an avant-garde art critic." Père Noël leaned down and stage-whispered, "We're talking about more than just subtitles. He likes art that has serious political and societal overtones."

"Uh oh. I was afraid of that." She wasn't sure what qualified as 'serious political and societal overtones,' but it sounded really boring. On that note, she yawned.

"Uncle, stop," Chris pleaded. "I'm trying to make a good impression here."

"I know, but Julianna deserves to know the truth." He reached over and rumpled his nephew's hair. "Beneath this slick, charming facade is a very sharp mind."

Slick and charming facade wasn't exactly how she'd have described Chris, but she was learning that he was full of surprises.

CHAPTER 8

Why did family always have to make things more difficult?

Chris shook his head. Here he was putting his best foot forward while his uncle was hell-bent on telling Jules the truth about him. In his experience, truth had no business in a new relationship. It should be discoverable after promises were made and vows taken. It wasn't lying so much as sugar-coating.

"I don't know about the avant-garde art thing. I went to an avant-garde art show once. The artist soaked cooked pasta in paint, hung canvas on the ceiling, and threw the pasta onto the canvas. Somehow it was supposed to signify the soul leaving the body and going to the after-life." The look on her face said she hadn't gotten the tie-in.

Now that he thought about it, neither did he.

"All I saw was colored pasta peeling off the canvas and dropping on people at the exhibit. I narrowly avoided a web of pink and black angel-hair." She hunched her shoulders. "Still don't get it."

Chris laughed at the mental image. "Yeah, how does pasta equate to the soul?"

"Exactly what I wanted to know. All it did was make me hungry for fettuccine alfredo."

She liked fettuccine alfredo. He filed that bit of info away for later use.

They walked toward the glowing red chateau. In spite of the evil red glow, it was peaceful here. A fresh dusting of snow covered everything. There was something contemplative about moonlight on snow.

Jules dropped to the ground, her arms and legs splayed out wide. She flapped them back and forth, making a snow angel. "I've always wanted to do this."

She'd never made a snow angel?

He lay on the ground and made his own snow angel. He loved Jules's energy and thirst for new experiences. Her excitement was infectious.

He sat up and a fast-moving ball of white smacked him directly in the nose.

So Jules wanted a snowball fight. It was on.

He scooped up snow and mashed it into a ball. He aimed for center mass and threw, but Jules dove out of the way.

"You kids have your fun. I'm going inside to make us something warm to drink." Père Noël waved.

Chris crunched together another snowball and hurled it at his uncle.

Père Noël snapped his fingers and the snowball melted before it got close to him.

Jules snapped her fingers and a green bucket full of snow dumped on Père Noël's head.

Chris's uncle laughed. "I didn't see that coming."

Chris glanced at Jules. "She's sneaky and beautiful. Lethal combination."

Jules looked confused by the beautiful comment.

He'd meant for her to be charmed, but all he got was confused. He'd never had this much trouble charming women before.

A snowball smacked her right cheek.

His uncle jumped up and down, clapping. "Never let your guard down."

"I deserve that." Jules dusted the snow off her face and then rubbed her hands together. "It's so cold."

He wondered where her gloves were. Probably back in the barn.

"How about we call a snowball truce and take my uncle up on his offer of something warm to drink?" Chris held out his hand.

She took it and laced her fingers through his. It was a small but intimate gesture. He was calling it a win. Her hands were freezing, but he didn't want to let go of her even long enough to warm her hands.

"Have you told her about Père Fouettard's hobby?" Père Noël nodded in the direction of his house.

"What hobby? It's not pickling little children is it?" Jules leaned close to Chris's ear. "I'm not eating any pork products while I'm here. In fact, I'd like to inspect all meat before I eat it. I don't mean to be a rude houseguest, but I'm not into eating the neighbor kids."

He never knew what was going to come out of her mouth next.

"I think the neighbor kids are safe. Père Fouettard has at least one good attribute—well, I guess two, since he loves Gui and she appears to love him back." He still couldn't wrap his mind around that one. "Fouettard restores antique carousels."

Jules's eyes narrowed while she processed that piece of information. "Yeah, I don't believe you." She put her hand over her heart. "I'm not calling you a liar, I'm just saying that you were given false information."

Père Noël opened the front door and stepped aside so Jules could see what was right inside.

Her mouth dropped open.

"I know ... right." Even after seeing the pictures of all of the restored carousels, Chris still couldn't believe that Père Fouettard was responsible for all of this beauty.

Jules unzipped her snowsuit and started to shrug it off but snapped her fingers instead. Now she wore a red sweater, jeans, and dark-brown fluffy boots.

He snapped his fingers and changed into a blue flannel shirt, jeans, and athletic shoes. Nothing said "I'm an approachable all-around great guy" like a flannel shirt. If it happened to match his eyes, that was just by accident.

"How old is this carousel?" Jules glanced at Père Noël as if for permission to go to it.

"I believe this one was built in 1832. And yes, of course you can touch it." Père Noël snapped his fingers and changed into black skinny jeans and a black sweatshirt.

Because he was tall and lanky, he looked like a human swizzle stick. Chris could now see that skinny jeans looked terrible on men. He swore off them right then and there.

Jules stepped onto the platform and went straight for a zebra. "I love all of the exotic animals. Usually it's just horses ... right?"

"Yes, most carousels, at least the original ones, are horses," Pére Noël said. "I've learned a lot about carousels over the years. The world's oldest carousel was completed in 1780. It's in Hanau-Wilhelmsbad State Park in Hanau, Germany. It had horses pulling chariots. Truly a lovely piece of art. It's currently being renovated. After Fouettard finishes with this one in a couple of weeks, he's going to take on that renovation."

"How does he renovate them without anyone noticing they're missing?" Jules looked around, taking it all in.

"The Spirit of Christmas gives him lots of help. It allows for an object to be in two places at once. The carousel is both here and there. Any progress the restorers make is reflected in this version, but Père Fouettard's work only shows up here. Then on Christmas Eve, the fully repaired carousel is revealed." Père Noël grinned like he was remembering a particularly good day. "Christmas miracles come in all shapes and sizes."

"Why doesn't Père Fouettard just snap his fingers and have the Spirit of Christmas restore it immediately?" Jules asked.

"The Spirit of Christmas could instantaneously restore the old carousel, but sometimes one must jump in and do things oneself. There is pride in accomplishment. If we relied only on the Christmas Spirit to do everything, we would lose our self-reliance."

Jules nodded. "I guess the same could be said for what I do. I suppose the Spirit of Christmas could heal Gui, but ... now that I think about it, why didn't the Spirit of Christmas heal Gui?"

"All animals need the human touch from time to time. The Spirit of Christmas probably could heal her and feed her, but it can't love her. Everyone and everything needs love. That is a uniquely human ability."

"That makes sense." Carefully, she ran her hand along the back of the zebra. "This is hand-carved wood. The Spirit of Christmas would have probably made this carving perfect. The imperfections are what make this carving personal." She nodded slowly. "I get it."

"I like the giraffe." Christ threw a leg over and mounted the carved giraffe.

Jules ran her hand over a tiger and then spotted a very

ornately carved carriage. It reminded Chris a lot of the gold carriage Queen Elizabeth trotted out for important queenly occasions.

"May I sit in this?" Jules pointed to the carriage. "I'd love a carousel ride. I rode on one once in New Braunfels when my group-home housemother took us to Wurstfest. The carousel wasn't free so I only got to ride once. I remember wishing that the carousel horses would dislodge their poles and take off running like they did in *Mary Poppins*."

Chris could feel the child's hope radiating off her in waves. Along with that hope was sadness and despair. He wished he could take the bad memories away, but all he could do was help her make new, good memories.

"Take a seat. I'm about to start her up. Everything works except for the music." Père Noël snapped his fingers and the carousel roared to life.

Light from the handblown glass bulbs danced off the inset mirrored and gilt scrollwork. Mutely the carousel traveled in a slow circle. The animals bobbed up and down. This was pure magic.

Jules giggled as she waved like Queen Elizabeth to all of her subjects. Jules's joy at something so ordinary as a carousel ride tore at Chris's heart. He wanted to give her every single experience she'd missed growing up.

He flapped the leather reins of his giraffe, pretending he could make it go faster.

Jules got up and made her way around the various animals until she threw a leg over the hippopotamus next to him.

She grabbed her reins. "Race you."

"You're on. The first one to make it all the way around wins." He leaned forward like a jockey trying to get his horse to bring home the win.

She did the same. "Henrietta Hippo here is faster than she looks."

He half expected their respective animals to trot off the carousel and take a lap around his uncle's warehouse-sized living room.

"Go, Henrietta, leave them in the dust." She giggled.

He could stand to hear that sound a billion more times.

"Oh, no, Geronimo the Giraffe refuses to come in second place. Giddyup, boy." He slapped his reins and kicked his heels into the wooden giraffe.

"I think Geronimo's a girl. She has the longest eyelashes I've ever seen on a giraffe." Jules kicked her heels and pointed to Geronimo's painted-on eyelashes.

Chris refused to be distracted. "You're just trying to divert my attention so you can win."

"Yep." She slapped her reins harder.

He'd never had so much fun fake-racing anyone.

"Okay, you two. It's time for hot chocolate." Père Noël held a tray in one hand and snapped the fingers of the other.

Slowly the carousel came to a stop.

Jules stepped off the carousel. "I don't suppose Père Fouettard would make me a miniature carousel for my apartment? Or the waiting room of my vet clinic?" Her eyes lit up. "It would be so fun to have my patients' humans ride it while I see their animals."

Her unadulterated joy should have made Chris happy, but her reference to her life outside of Christmas, Texas, was a constant reminder of what she would have to give up if they were going to be together. But he was getting ahead of himself. He was ready to skip to the end even though they'd barely started.

His uncle handed Jules a red mug. Little swirls of steam wafted up. She sniffed the mug. "This smells amazing." She took a sip and swooned. "This just might be the best thing I've ever tasted."

"It's sipping chocolate, the French version of hot chocolate." Père Noël grinned. "So glad you like it. It's my own special recipe … centuries in the making."

She put her arm around Père Noël. "I've only got one question …"

"Yes, I'll give you the recipe." His uncle was so honored and pleased that Jules liked his hot chocolate.

"Oh, no, I don't want the recipe. I'm not kitchen compatible." She took another sip and swallowed. "I just want to know if you're married. And if not, do you want to be?"

Chris put his hands on his hips. "Now wait a minute."

She'd met his uncle like fifteen minutes ago, and she was proposing?

Chris would make a better mug of hot chocolate. He'd dedicate his life to doing it.

His uncle laughed. "No, I'm single." He winked at Chris. "I think there may be someone else interested in a future with you."

Chris could feel his cheeks burning.

Jules turned to Chris and studied him. "Really?"

Chris opened his mouth, but nothing came out. Was it possible to be embarrassed into speechlessness?

As if in slow motion, Jules leaned up on her tippy-toes and kissed Chris lightly on the lips.

Chris's hands went to her shoulders pulling her closer.

His chest knocked into her hot chocolate mug, and hot liquid sloshed down the front of her sweater. She screamed and jumped back, pulling at her sweater as rivulets of hot liquid almost burned her chest.

Père Noël snapped his fingers and her sweater dried.

Jules patted her chest gingerly as if checking it for burns.

Chris wasn't sure if it was okay to pull her in for another

hug, so he dropped his hands before they made it to her shoulders. "I'm so sorry."

She nodded. "I'm fine, but I think it's safe to say that was the worst first kiss ever."

Chris wanted to crawl under a huge rock and stay there for the next couple of centuries.

His uncle threw back his head and laughed until tears ran down his cheeks.

"I'm glad my horrible embarrassment and Jules's possible third-degree burns are so amusing." Chris had the almost overwhelming desire to punch his second-favorite uncle.

Père Noël held up a hand as he doubled over, crying with laughter. "I'm sorry, it's just hilarious."

Jules watched Père Noël as if waiting for the punch line.

Finally, his uncle got the laughter under control and dried his eyes with his sleeve. "I'm sorry, I couldn't help myself."

Chris put his arm around Jules. He half expected her to flinch, but she only leaned in to him.

"I don't understand, what's so funny?"

Chris shook his head. "No idea."

"I'm guessing your father and mother never told you how they met?" His uncle grinned.

"They met at a county fair or something. How's that funny?" Chris was fairly certain his uncle had lost his mind. It was probably living with Fouettard all of these centuries. The evil had finally rubbed off on him.

"Your father was an apprentice carpenter who made his way to the city of Myra, trying to find work. Our father was a master carpenter and had taught us well, but he'd died several months before. There was no work in the village where we lived, so your father and most of my brothers set off in different directions, trying to find work. I went with my older brother, Titus Lucius." His uncle smiled at the memory. "You know him as Santa Claus."

Père Noël nodded toward the kitchen table close to the fire.

Chris kept his arm around Jules and then held the chair out for her to sit.

"Thanks." Jules smiled up at him as he helped her scoot the chair under the table.

Chris sat next to her and debated putting his arm around her again but decided it might be too much too soon.

Jules propped her chin on her fist. "So Santa traveled to Myra to find work."

She was into the story. He could feel her excitement and eagerness to hear the rest of the story. Was it because she'd never had a family that made her thirsty for family history?

It was strange that Chris had never heard the whole story about how his parents had met. Or maybe he had but he'd forgotten. Unlike Jules, he'd grown up with a family, so familial history hadn't been that important.

"The town of Myra was having some sort of trade fair or something. I can't remember what exactly, but everyone was outside. Booths were set up with vendors selling everything from spices to jewelry to fish. Myra was a port city ... very successful and very cosmopolitan for its time." Père Noël waved it away. "I remember it being night. Titus and I made our way to the amphitheater. I remember thinking that it was the most impressive structure I'd ever seen. There were rows and rows of seats carved out of the granite hillside. My brother traded a torchbearer a little carved deer for a torch. They were making the exchange when your father backed into your mother, making her drop the basket of fish she was trying to sell. He turned around, took one look at her, and promptly dropped the torch. It caught the bottom of your mother's palla on fire."

Jules looked like she was soaking it all in. "What's a palla?"

"It was a mantle or shawl-like piece of clothing women

wore back then." Père Noël laughed at the memory. "He ripped the palla off her shoulder and stamped out the fire. Unfortunately, he managed also to trample all of the fish she was trying to sell." He smiled. "She told your father that since he'd destroyed all of her fish, which she'd been going to use the money from to buy food, he now owed her a very nice meal, and it had better not be fish."

"To this day, Mom won't eat fish. She hates it." Chris was getting into the story.

"My brother used what little coinage we had to buy a loaf of bread, some sort of meat—I don't remember what—and some fruits and vegetables." His uncle turned to Jules. "There weren't restaurants like we have today. There were taverns and inns where you could buy a meal, but they were dirty and mainly used for prostitution. A tavern was no place for a respectable female, so your mother took us back to her house and made us the best food I'd ever tasted. That was the first time I'd ever had basil. She'd infused olive oil with it, and we dipped our bread in it." His uncle's face showed that he was lost in the memory. "Your father offered to marry her that evening. He had no idea if she had a dowry, and he didn't care. All he'd ever wanted for himself was her."

Jules reached out and covered Père Noël's hand with hers. "That is a beautiful story. I can see it in my mind. I can't wait to Google the town of Myra. I'd love to see it." She patted his hand and then leaned back in her chair. "Why didn't you ever marry?"

His uncle smiled. "Believe it or not, we magical beings have a hard time finding love. E-Harmony doesn't have a category for mythical figures with eternal life. I've had my chance a time or two, but I never found a person I loved the way your father loves your mother. Even now, centuries later, they still enjoy each other's company."

Jules nodded. "Santa and Mrs. Claus really do enjoy each

other. When I was little, I wished for parents like them. I have no idea who my father was, and I don't remember my mother, but I would invent these stories about them. You know, like they were some sort of *Romeo and Juliet* forbidden love story, or they were spies who thought it was safer to leave me with strangers than it was for me to live with them."

Chris could feel the sadness and desperate need to belong coming off Jules. He wanted as desperately for her to belong to him.

CHAPTER 9

Jules loved hearing about Chris's family, but she could barely keep her eyes open. It was hard to believe she was sitting at a table talking to someone who'd been a citizen of the Roman Empire.

Jules yawned and stretched, but she wasn't ready to go. She loved hearing about the past, especially stories that involved family history. When she'd been small and alone and needed to feel like she belonged somewhere, she'd make up these fantasies about how she was descended from the Egyptian pharaohs or was the great-great-great-grandniece of Laura Ingalls Wilder or maybe the great-great-granddaughter of a gin-guzzling flapper.

As long as she didn't know where she came from, anything was possible. She'd always tried to convince herself that was a good thing. A little mystery never hurt anyone. Only, it had hurt … deeply … to not know from whom she'd come. She had no family history. She had no one to claim as her own.

Even now as a fully grown and self-aware adult, it still felt like something was missing.

Why was this coming up now? She'd let it go years ago. So what if she was raised in the foster care system? So were thousands of other kids, and they weren't whining about not having a family. It must be exhaustion, because she was never this whiny.

She scooted back from the table. "I'd love to hear more stories in the morning, but I need to get some sleep."

She glanced in the direction of the barn. "I should go check on Gui."

Père Noël covered her hand with his. "Chris, will you go check on her? I'd like to talk to Julianna alone."

Chris looked at Jules, waiting for her to give him the okay to leave her alone. He worried about her. It was kind of him. She nodded. She was bone-tired.

Père Noël watched Chris leave the kitchen and waited until the front door opened and closed.

He took both of her hands in his. "Oh, my dear child. You have such a big heart, and I hate that it's been broken so many times. I could tell you that family doesn't make you the person you are, but that's a lie. Family is important. Those of us who are fortunate enough to have grown up in a loving one take that for granted. I have lived for a very long time, and I can tell you that my family has gotten me through the tough times as well as the happy times. My parents are long dead and gone, but I remember them every day. I've outlived my three sisters, and I always thought losing them was hard, but now I see that never having known them would have been so much worse."

If she allowed herself to cry, tears would be rolling down her cheeks, but she had given up childish tears a long time ago. She wanted to tell Père Noël that she didn't care and that she'd made her own sort of family, but she couldn't get the words out.

"Would you like to know about your biological parents? I

believe I can show them to you." Gently, he squeezed her hands. "I can tell you that you have no living blood family."

Finally, after all of these years, she had the chance to find out about her family. But they were all dead. There was zero chance of connecting with them. Did she really want to know about them?

Père Noël had just said that mourning the loss of his sisters was better than not knowing them at all. She had to know. It was more than just her curious nature; something deep inside of her needed to know why they'd given her away.

Jules took a deep breath and let it out slowly. "Yes, I think I'd like to know."

Père Noël closed his eyes and then snapped his fingers.

Jules looked around for some sort of secret government file or dossier of some kind, or at least some pictures of her parents, but nothing popped into existence.

A loud thump came from behind the door to the left of the enormous stove. The door burst open and out came Santa.

"Really, Septimus? Can't you just call me like a normal brother? You have a cell phone." Santa hugged his brother.

Père Noël used his forearm to shield his eyes. "You really need to get a tan on those glow-in-the-dark white legs. The glare is blinding."

Santa rolled his eyes. "Grooming advice from a grown man wearing skinny jeans." He swept Jules up in a hug. "How are you, my dear? You look tired."

"I am." Jules was more than tired; she was weary. "I thought you couldn't leave Christmas, Texas, or the Spirit of Christmas would die."

Santa winked at her. "Just like the carousels Père Fouettard repairs, I am both here and there."

She laughed. Leave it to Santa Claus to make her laugh during a huge personal crisis.

"Our Julianna would like to find out more about her blood family." Père Noël pulled up a chair for his older brother.

Santa took the seat. "You realize that's against the rules."

"What rules? It's not like St. Nicholas dropped a couple of rock tablets in our laps with the Spirit of Christmas commandments." Père Noël was different around his brother.

Was that what it was like to have a sibling? She'd always wanted one.

"Now that I think about it, Julianna did wish one Christmas to find out about her family, so technically, it isn't against the rules." Santa took one of Jules's hands.

Père Noël took the other. "Close your eyes."

"This feels oddly séance-y." Jules closed her eyes anyway.

The palms of her hands heated, and she felt herself falling. She landed in a sparse one-room apartment. She sniffed the air. It smelled like bacon and apple pie.

A thin, auburn-haired girl picked up a squirming bundle from a ratty old stroller and cradled the bundle close. "There's my Julie-bug … Mommy loves you so much. By next week, I should have enough money from my tips at the diner downstairs to buy you a secondhand crib. I'm sorry you have to sleep in this old stroller, but someday we're going to live in a real house with a backyard and everything. You're going to have tons of toys, and I'll make us breakfast on a real stove instead of this hot plate. We're going to have a wonderful life together, my Julie bug. I promise."

Jules memorized her mother's face. Her mother had wanted and loved her. It shouldn't have mattered, but it did. Jules wanted to sit down with the woman and tell her that everything had worked out. Her Julie-bug had made something of herself.

Time seemed to speed up. Her mother was a little older now, and the baby was now a full-grown toddler. They still lived in the same apartment, but now there was a small TV and the floor was littered with toys.

Her mother picked her up and tried to brush her hair, but Julie squirmed out of her mother's arms. "Come on now, Julie-bug. I want you to look your best to meet your father."

Julie giggled as she hugged her favorite toy, a pink bunny, and ran from her mother. Her mother laughed and scooped Julie up and gave her loud kisses on her cheeks. "Okay, my sweet baby girl, you need to help Mommy remember not to give your father any money. He promised he's given up meth, but I've heard that before. He asked to meet you and I can't say no. No matter how bad his problems are, he's still your father. We're meeting him across town. It's best if he doesn't know where we live."

Jules felt herself falling, and when she opened her eyes she was back in Père Noël's kitchen.

"Wait, but I was about to meet my father." Jules slammed her eyes shut. "Take me back. I want to meet my father."

She waited for them to take her to meet her father, but nothing happened. She waited a couple more beats and then opened her eyes.

She glanced from Santa to Père Noël and back to Santa. "Take me back, please. I want to see my father."

Père Noël shook his head. "We can't."

"I don't understand. I'd like to see my father." Why would they show her her mother but not her father?

Pain etched across Santa's face. She'd never seen him anything but jolly. "I'm sorry, child, but I refuse to show you the rest. I won't do it."

"Why?" This was beyond strange. Why take her only part of the way?

Santa squeezed her hand. "What did they tell you about your mother's death?"

Jules shrugged. "Not much, only that she died when I was a baby."

She'd always imagined that her mother had died from some sort of illness, but a bad feeling slithered in the pit of her stomach. She needed to know the truth. "How did she die?"

Santa studied the table like he was gathering the courage to tell her something awful.

He stiffened his spine and sat forward. "Your father was addicted to crystal methamphetamine. When your mother refused to give him any money, he pulled out a knife and stabbed her. She died shortly after. She loved you and wanted you. Your father did too, but the drugs ate away his mind. You were loved and are loved. You belonged to a beautiful mother who loved you from the minute she found out she was carrying you."

"You were her Julie-bug and she adored you." Père Noël wiped away the tears rolling down his cheeks. "I wish you could feel how much she loved you. Her love for you was like a warm ray of sunshine on a cold, cloudy day. She lit up from the inside when she was around you. Her name was Alice McCowan, and you were her world."

Jules felt the dam break as tears rolled down her cheeks. She couldn't and wouldn't hold them back any longer. She had been loved by her mother whose name was Alice. She had a loving mother who'd wanted her. She wasn't alone anymore. She could feel her mother with her. All of the tears she'd denied herself came out in a desperate cry. She could feel Julianna coming back and staking her claim on the mother who'd loved her.

Santa patted her back. "Oh, my lovely child. I hate that you grew up thinking you weren't loved. I hate that. I should have done better. I should have showed you sooner how much your mother loved you."

She felt Santa's hand drop away. "I did save this for you."

She wiped her eyes and looked up.

He was holding her tattered, old pink bunny. She'd thrown it away all those years ago when she'd given up wanting a family.

"Commander Bun Bun." Jules took the bunny and hugged it to her. She brought it up to her nose. "It still smells the same." She turned it over and the ratty, white, silky tag was still there. When she'd been really scared, she'd used the tag to self-soothe by rolling it between her thumb and index finger. She did that now. The tag still rolled up into a thin tube.

She threw her arms around Santa and hugged him tight. "Thank you for saving Commander Bun Bun. I thought I'd never see her again."

She dropped her arms and moved to Père Noël. She threw her arms around him. "Thank you for knowing exactly what I needed right when I needed it."

Père Noël smiled broadly. "You are so special, Julianna." He kissed her forehead. "I love you, my sweet child. You love so deeply and thoroughly that nothing stands in your way." He turned to his brother. "She's even charmed Père Fouettard. Not only did she make him back down, but he's actually doing what she told him to do."

Santa's mouth dropped open. "I don't believe it. Fouettard never backs down, and he certainly isn't known for following instructions."

Jules laughed even through the tears running down her cheeks. She pointed to the carousel. "He's not all bad. He restores these beautiful carousels and he loves Gui. Animal lovers are good people in my book."

"Wow. I've never met anyone besides St. Nicholas who thought of Fouettard as a good person." Santa beamed at her. "You're so special, Julie-bug."

She loved hearing that name, Julie-bug. It was probably a bad idea to change her first name to Julie-bug, but she was going to insist that her close friends call her that.

She took each man's hand and squeezed them lightly. "Thank you both for this wonderful gift. I know it's strange, but I can feel her with me. She's always been with me, I know that now."

Santa and Père Noël shared a look.

Santa squeezed her hand back. "I know this is a terrible time, but I need to ask you for a favor."

Jules dried her eyes and nodded enthusiastically. "Anything. I'm happy to help you with anything. Is another animal sick?"

Santa shook his head. "No, all magical animals that I know of are fine except for Gui, who I hear is recovering. No, this is about my son Chris. He's in love with you."

"Are you sure?" She didn't see it.

He was nervous around her. Was that a sign of love? She'd never been in love before, so she couldn't say. But if the Hollywood rom-com was anywhere close to the truth, nerves really weren't part of the deal. Now angst … that was a different story.

"I try not to interfere too much in my sons' lives," Santa continued, " but I'm stepping in now. I don't want him hurt, so if you find that you don't return his feelings, I need for you to let him know soon."

She owed Santa so much. He wanted his son to be happy, so she would do her best to repay him by exploring a relationship with his son. It was the least she could do.

"No, Julianna. Gratitude has no place in love. You can't make yourself love someone. That isn't fair to you or them. If you can't give Chris your heart freely because you love him, you need to tell him that. He deserves to find someone who loves him as much as he loves them." He squeezed her hand again. "All I want is for you to be open to the idea of love. You can't decide to love someone. Either you do or you don't."

She enjoyed spending time with Chris, but she barely knew him. There was something there, but it was too early to label it.

She nodded. "I promise to be open to the idea, and if I can't return his feelings, I'll let him know."

It felt like she had the weight of the world on her shoulders.

"Oh my God. What have the two of you done?" Chris ran over to Jules and put his arm around her. "Why is she crying?"

Chris was protective of her. Why hadn't she noticed that before? It was nice. Yes, there was definitely something there.

She winked at Santa. "Oh yeah, there's something there."

He returned her wink. "Take all the time you need."

Chris shot them both a curious look as he pulled her into a hug and patted her back. "Shh now. Whatever they did, I'm going to make them stop. They had better apologize right now or I'm telling Mom."

"Now hold on a minute, son. Let's not get your mother involved." Santa turned all cajoling and contrite.

"Let's leave Nell out of this. What she doesn't know won't hurt us." Père Noël actually sounded a little bit frightened.

Jules laughed. "One mention of Mrs. Claus and they both sound scared. Remind me to ask her how she keeps her men in line. She's such a sweet, kind soul. I didn't know she had a dark side."

"It's not dark so much as disappointing. Disappointing her is a fate worse than death." Père Noël made it sound really bad.

"You two have some serious explaining to do. Why did you upset Jules? And why aren't the two of you apologizing—"

"They didn't upset me. They introduced me to my mother." Jules wiped her cheeks. "She was amazing and she loved me so much. We didn't have much, but I could feel how much she loved me." Still loves me, Jules thought. Still loves me. It seemed that love crossed over all planes of existence.

Chris glanced at his father and then his uncle. "Introduced her to her mother … I don't understand."

"They took me back in time and let me see her with me when I was a baby." Why did these past few minutes finally make her feel like she belonged?

"That's against the rules." Chris eyed his father. "How are you here and the world hasn't imploded because you're not in Christmas, Texas?"

His father winked. "I was never here." He snapped his fingers and then he was gone.

Jules laughed and held out her hand. It was time to reintroduce Julianna to the world. "Hello, Chris, it's nice to meet you. My name is Julianna, but you can call me Julie or Jules or Julie-bug."

Chris took her hand and kissed the palm. "The pleasure's all mine."

His kiss sent a tingle up her spine. There was something there all right. There was attraction, and that was definitely a start.

CHAPTER 10

Chris didn't have a lot of experience with crying women, but he knew he'd never liked seeing anyone cry. Now he felt helpless to make Jules ... Julie ... feel better.

It was strange. He wasn't getting sadness off of her, he was getting bone-deep happiness, which didn't explain the tears. He'd never understood the tears-of-joy thing.

"I think it's time for you to go to bed." He nodded in the direction of the front door. "I checked on Gui and she's sleeping soundly. Fouettard covered her with a blanket like she's a tiny little lapdog. He said to thank you. I had to pinch myself just to make sure it wasn't a dream. I've never heard him thank anyone."

Père Noël stood. "I can tell you he's never thanked anyone, including St. Nicholas for not killing him on the spot after he resurrected those three boys."

"I wish I could act all humble, but I'm pretty impressed with myself. I've had lots of practice not backing down. When I first opened my practice, I had lots of people—both men and women—who thought I was too young to know anything about healing animals. They used to talk over me, or even worse, try to put me in my place, but I never backed down. I had to earn their respect. It's taught me confidence the hard way." She smiled and she exuded an easy confidence.

She yawned.

"You two should get some sleep." Père Noël nodded in the direction of the steep staircase off to one corner of the living room. "I'll show you to your rooms."

Chris put his hand in the small of Julie's back and led her to the staircase.

They all clomped up the stairs.

When they stepped on the upstairs landing, Père Noël opened the first door on the right. "This is for you, Julie-bug."

Her eyes went huge. "OMG, this is the coolest room ever." She pointed to the huge four-poster bed complete with wooden canopy. "That's beautiful."

Père Noël grinned. "Thank you. It took me ten years to build it."

"You made this bed?" Julie's voice was all awe.

"Yes, I come from a long line of master carpenters." Chris's uncle pointed to the door across from the bed. "The bathroom's in there. Just snap your fingers if you need anything."

Julie wrapped her arms around him. "Thank you for everything."

"You are very welcome, Julie-bug." He patted her on the back and then stepped back.

"What about me?" Chris tried not to sound needy, but it was hard. "Where's my hug?"

"Why do you get a hug?" Julie was all seriousness.

His heart sank until he saw her eyes twinkle. She was messing with him.

"I drove you here and fed you. That's got to be worth something." He held his arms out wide, waiting for his hug.

"I guess it's okay since I'm not holding any hot liquids." She stepped into his arms and hugged him.

"Hey, that was a onetime deal." He hoped.

She felt good against him, and there was something different about her now. He couldn't put his finger on it.

She dropped her arms and seemed to be waiting for him to drop his, but he held on.

She said something but her voice was muffled against his chest.

He loosened the slack a bit but didn't let her go. "What did you say?"

"I said that we deserve a first-kiss do-over." She smiled up at him.

She raised up on her tippy-toes while he leaned down. She closed her eyes and he closed his. This was going to be the best first kiss of his life. He opened his mouth slightly in the hope that their first kiss would be less chaste. He leaned down even more and finally connected with her … nose. He startled back and chin-butted her in the forehead.

"Ouch." Her hands went to her forehead.

"Oh no, did I hurt you?" How could their first-kiss redo be worse than the actual first kiss?

"Just a little." She waved him away with her free hand, while her other hand massaged her forehead. "You have a very bony chin."

"You two are appallingly bad at this." His uncle shook his head. "I remember kissing being easier and with less bodily harm."

Chris no longer wanted to hide under a rock. Now he wanted the earth to swallow him up.

Julie started laughing. Pretty soon she was doubled over and tears were once again running down her cheeks. This was definitely not the tears-of-joy thing. It was all tears of hilarity.

"What's so funny?" He should slink away in defeat to his room, but Julie deserved a man with a backbone.

"Our first kisses just keep getting worse. I'm afraid I'll suffer a broken bone with the next one." She was laughing so hard it looked like she could barely breathe.

His heart shrank to the size of a pebble. He wanted to disagree with her, but she had a point. Clearly, they weren't meant to be together.

"Might I make a suggestion?" his uncle said from behind him.

At this point Chris had nothing to lose. "Of course."

"Skip over the first kiss and move on to just kissing." Père Noël laughed. "Just remember that the Spirit of Christmas can heal broken bones, so I think you'll be okay." He winked and left the room, closing the door behind him.

Julie laughed, leaned up, and gave Chris a loud, smacking kiss on the lips.

Gently, he pulled her into him and kissed her back with all of the love he felt for her. She melted against him and opened her mouth. His tongue darted in and she moaned. He pressed her closer to him.

Oh yes, they had kissing down.

He ended the kiss and hugged her tightly to him.

He glanced over to where Pere Noel had been, but the man had slipped out.

Julie mumbled something against his chest and he loosened his hold.

She looked dazed and flushed. He'd put that red on her cheeks. The caveman part of his brain wanted to grunt in victory, kill a brontosaurus, and cook it for her dinner. The rest of his brain wanted to kiss her again.

"Wow." Her eyes were still closed. "Where did you learn to kiss like that?"

"I'm over sixteen hundred years old. I've picked up a few things here and there." Male pride almost gave in to the caveman, but he was fresh out of brontosauruses.

And they both needed sleep.

Reluctantly, he dropped his arms and stepped back.

"You need sleep and so do I." All he wanted was her.

"You're going to kiss me like that and then leave?" She shook her head. "I don't understand men. Y'all say we're the complicated ones."

"I'm quitting while I'm ahead." He loved that she wanted more of him.

"That's just dumb." She motioned to the bed. "It's more than big enough for two."

The breath caught in his throat, and it was his turn to be dazed and flushed.

"Not tonight." His voice cracked, so he cleared it. "You're tired and I prefer a well-rested lover."

"It's your loss." She snapped her fingers. Her sweater and jeans disappeared. She stood there in the teeny-tiniest excuse for underwear he'd ever seen and a matching black lace bra. Gone were her boots. They'd been replaced by the highest black heels he'd ever seen.

His mouth actually watered.

"Too bad. I'm going to take a long, hot bath." She turned around to give him the rear view of her tiny panties.

His heart stopped beating and he forgot to breathe. Black lace barely covered her backside.

She tried to strut, but clearly she wasn't used to heels, because her legs wobbled. She glanced at him over her shoulder as she threw open the closet door and strut-wobbled inside. "Oh crap, this isn't the bathroom."

He had no choice but to laugh.

"Love, it's the other door." The "love" had slipped out. He hoped she didn't think it was awkward.

She poked her head out and grinned. "I had a fifty-fifty shot and blew it. Also, I need to take these shoes off before I break my ankle."

"I'll leave you to your bath." He wanted to stay more than he wanted to breathe, but he wanted more from her than just sex. He had to concentrate on walking just to make his legs move. Once he made it to the door, he turned around. "I'll be right across the hall if you need me."

More than anything, he really wanted her to need something. He didn't have the willpower to look at her and still be able to leave; he didn't look back as he closed the door.

His uncle waited in the hallway. "I think you should have stayed."

"It's not the right time." Chris had never thought of himself as old-fashioned, but here he was wanting the vows to take place before the bedding.

Père Noël opened the door across the hall and held it open for Chris.

They walked inside the cozy room decorated in different shades of blue.

"She has feelings for you." His uncle sat on the sofa close to the fireplace.

"I'm not so sure she wants more than friendship." Although she'd wanted more than friendship just now.

"She does, and not starting tonight. She has feelings for you that she couldn't see until now." His uncle crossed his legs. "She lacked confidence in love."

Chris had felt that. That was what was different about her. She now knew that her mother had loved her and wanted her. She hadn't been abandoned.

He sat next to his uncle. Something had been bothering him since his father had asked for privacy for he and Julie.

"Are you sure that's all there is to it? I have the feeling that my father might have put something subconscious in her head about me."

"Are you talking about the moment where he asked you to give them privacy?" His uncle laughed. "That was about you, but it had nothing to do with her feelings about you or yours about her. Completely separate matter."

Chris didn't believe his uncle, but he knew from experience that the man could keep a confidence no matter what. In fact, Père Noël had kept several confidences about Chris that even Chris's mother couldn't get out of his uncle.

Père Noël rose. "You need to get some sleep. You and Julie have a big day tomorrow. You're going to teach her how to ski."

"Are you sure Dad didn't have anything to do with Julie and me?" Chris really wanted for her to choose him because she wanted him and not because his father had interfered.

"I promise. I can't tell you what they talked about, but you'll find out soon." His uncle walked to the door. "Sleep well."

He closed the door.

Chris couldn't shake the feeling that he and Julie weren't in this relationship alone.

CHAPTER 11

Jules hadn't been prepared for that kiss. She was more than a little attracted to Chris. Now that she thought about it, that attraction had always been there.

He was in love with her. She smiled at the thought, but then why was she sleeping in this huge bed alone?

She frowned. Santa wanted her to let Chris down if she couldn't return his feelings. That was a lot of pressure. She had feelings for Chris, but she wasn't sure if it was love.

Clearly, Chris was old-fashioned and didn't want to rush things. But she was a rush-into-things kind of person. Maybe they should take it slow. She didn't want to hurt Chris. The thought of hurting him actually made her nauseated.

No, they needed to take it slow.

Chris was definitely old-fashioned, and he had a right to be. He was old . . . really old. She laughed. So did that make her his much younger trophy wife?

She could get behind that idea.

Secretly, she'd always thought that she could out-trophy-wife with the best of them. Except she'd have to marry some old dude. With Chris she had the best of both worlds—she could be a trophy wife and he would stay young and handsome forever.

She snapped her fingers and the bedside lamp went off. She'd been too tired for a long, hot bath, so she'd quickly showered and gone to bed.

"Goodnight, Commander Bun Bun." She reached for the stuffed animal on the nightstand and kissed her goodnight. She set Bun Bun back on the nightstand and noticed a strange glow coming from the top drawer. She opened it to find an overly large snow globe.

It was odd. There was nothing in the center. No snowy village or figure-skating ice princess or even Santa or Père Noël. She shook it and fake snow fluttered down on the emptiness that should have held some sort of winter scene.

She yawned and put the snow globe on the nightstand next to the Commander.

In seconds, she was sound asleep.

She had the feeling of falling again, just like she'd had when Père Noël and Santa had shown her the past. She fell slower and slower until she landed on the bottom of something. It was white, but not snowy white. It was like a huge empty white stage of some sort.

She stood and looked around, getting her bearings. There was a very bright light above her. It was like the whole ceiling was a giant convex movie screen. She heard laughter and then an image of her came into view.

She was laughing. The image panned out, and she could see herself wearing a simple white sundress, holding a handful of butter-yellow roses, and holding the arm of Père Fouettard. They were walking down a soft, grassy lane that was bordered with fields of wildflowers in every shade of the rainbow. She was happy, really happy. She glowed with it.

Jules or well, Julie—she was going back to Julie—watched

as she and Fouettard made their way to a blond man wearing a simple blue button-down and khakis. It was Chris. He smiled down at her and offered her his arm.

They walked a little farther to a grotto where two large, wild, pink rosebushes intertwined, creating an arbor. They turned to each other and held hands.

Julie smiled up at Chris and said, "I promise to love you forever, to put your happiness before mine, and to take you as my husband for now and for every tomorrow after." She leaned up and kissed him on the cheek.

Chris smiled down at her. "I promise to love you forever, to put your happiness above my own, and to take you as my wife for now and for every tomorrow after." He leaned down and kissed her on the cheek.

As Julie watched, it occurred to her that this was her wedding. There was no minister and no rings exchanged and no pomp and circumstance, only the promises she and Chris made to each other. It was perfect—exactly what she'd never allowed herself to want.

"The future's not set," a quiet male voice said from behind her. There was something both familiar and calming in his voice. "There's no fate but what we make for ourselves."

She turned around to find a regal-looking old man with white hair and a mischievous gleam in his eyes. She was willing to bet that when he babysat his grandkids he let them eat M&M's for dinner and wash them down with Dr Pepper.

He was a stranger, but she felt like she knew him.

"Aren't you going to ask who I am?" The man smiled.

"No, you'll tell me if you want me to know. I've already decided you're a friend." Being around him made her feel loved. "Anyone who quotes the *Terminator* is good people."

He let out a loud, rumbling laugh and swept his hand up, indicating the ceiling. "We're inside the snow globe and we're looking at your future. Or the future you might have. If you choose it. It is a choice you have to make freely and for love."

She nodded. "I know. I can feel it."

"Would you like to see the rest?" He pointed to the ceiling.

"The rest of my future? How long is it going to take?" She really needed to wake Chris up and convince him to marry her. She knew down to the bone. He was her other half.

"No, just a little taste of what's to come." He snapped his fingers and they were falling again.

They landed gracefully—well, he landed gracefully and she landed facedown. She rolled over, laced her fingers behind her head, crossed her legs at the ankle, and looked overhead.

A little girl of about five was seat-belted in the back seat of a truck. The little girl had auburn, curly hair, huge blue eyes, and a mischievous smile. Commander Bun Bun was strapped into the seat next to her.

"Mommy, why can't Daddy come with us when we go help sick animals?" The little girl leaned forward to look at the driver.

The scene panned out, and Julie saw that she was the driver.

She sat up. "Mommy? She called me Mommy. I'm her mommy."

An overwhelming sense of love crashed through her. She loved this little girl with everything she had in her. She reached up as if she could touch the little girl, but of course that wasn't possible.

"Well, Daddy can't leave Christmas, Texas. He has to stay with Santa to keep the Spirit of Christmas alive." Her older self laughed. "Also, I don't think he likes watching animals give birth. Now that I have you and you have his gift of compassion and can talk to the animals, he doesn't need to come along."

"I like talking to the animals. Sometimes they think the silliest things. I can't wait to meet Apple Sauce's new calf." The little girl genuinely loved working with animals, just like Julie.

"I'm going to call you Alice, Queen of the Animals, from now on." Her older self looked at her daughter in the rearview mirror.

Alice. Their daughter's name was Alice.

Alice's eyes went huge. "Do I get to wear a crown?"

"Absolutely, every queen needs a crown. The more rhinestones the better." Older Julie watched the road.

Alice snapped her fingers and a huge rhinestone tiara appeared on her little head.

"Hey, we talked about snappy-fingering outside of Christmas. You can't do it in public. You promised." Her older self was in serious mommy mode.

"I know. St. Nicholas says snappy-fingering outside Christmas is okay in an emergency." Alice was all seriousness. "I needed my crown."

Julie couldn't argue with a crown emergency. She turned to the old man.

"You're St. Nicholas." Julie smiled up at him. "Thank you for always watching out for me."

She had very vivid memories of him kneeling next to her bed and comforting her when she'd felt so alone.

He smiled. "My child, you're one of my favorites, just as your daughter is. A crown emergency … that's adorable."

He pulled her in for a hug. "I wish I could have saved your mother, but there are limits to what I can do. You're right, she is always with you. A mother's love is without measure, as you will soon find out. Chris is a good man and he's your destiny, but you still have a choice. Love isn't a responsibility or an obligation."

"I know." She wanted this life, and she wanted Chris. "I want to make a family with him."

"He's the best of men." St. Nicholas nodded. "Just so you know, Gui is fine. She's fully healed, thanks to you." He laughed. "You won over Fouettard. I have to say that I didn't see that one coming. That man is very complicated, but you bring out the best in him. Just remember, everyone is redeemable, even him."

Something occurred to her. "Why does everyone speak English? I know it's supposed to be the language of business, but shouldn't you or Fouettard have an accent?"

"You're a smart one. The easy answer is that we don't speak English, you just hear it." He leaned in close and whispered, "Remember the universal translator from *Galaxy Quest?*"

Her mouth dropped open. "I knew that movie was real."

The old man put his hand on her arm and they were falling again.

Julie sat up. Sunlight streamed in from the windows on the left. She glanced at the nightstand. The snow globe was there next to Commander Bun Bun, but the snow globe was no longer empty. Inside was a miniature rhinestone tiara just like the one Alice would wear.

"Thank you, St. Nicholas. I hope to see you again soon." She could swear she felt his hand on her shoulder.

Julie threw back the covers and ran across the hall. She didn't bother knocking but just burst into the room.

Chris sat bolt upright. "What's wrong?"

He rubbed his eyes. Clearly, she'd woken him up.

He looked her up and down and then his eyes locked onto her bare legs.

She glanced down at her Darth Vader Christmas T-shirt with the quote, "I find your lack of Christmas Spirit disturbing."

Okay, so maybe she should have snappy-fingered some clothes. She raised her hand to do just that.

"Don't. I'm enjoying the view." Chris grinned. "I didn't know Darth Vader was such a huge fan of Christmas."

"Thank God you recognize him. That's a sign that what I'm about to do is the right thing." Julie got down on one knee. "Will you marry me?"

Chris's mouth dropped open. A full minute passed.

Her heart sank. "It's okay. I understand." She stood and started to back out of the room.

Chris was up and pulling her into a hug before she'd made it to the door.

"Yes, I'll marry you, but I wanted to be the one to ask." Chris kissed her.

She returned the kiss with all the love in her heart.

Chris hugged her to him. "Will you marry me?"

"I thought you'd never ask." She hugged him tight.

"Now that you've said yes and we're officially engaged, I want your promise that nothing will ever tear us apart." He was all seriousness.

"Okay." It sounded serious. She was starting to get worried.

"There's something I need to tell you." He was somber.

"What?" Oh my God, was he dying? Wait, didn't he have eternal life? "If it's bad, we'll work through it together. Together we can conquer anything. There is nothing you can tell me that will make me fall out of love with you."

"I hate *Star Wars*. I've seen all of the movies and hated every single one." He grinned.

She just laughed. "Oh, that is a problem."

ABOUT THE AUTHOR

Katie Graykowski is an award-winning author who likes sassy heroines, Mexican food, movies where lots of stuff gets blown up, and glitter nail polish. She lives on a hilltop outside of Austin, Texas where her home office has an excellent view of the Texas Hill Country. When she's not writing, she's scuba diving. Drop by her website www.katiegraykowski.com or send her an email at katiegraykowski@me.com.

www.ingramcontent.com/pod-product-compliance
Ingram Content Group UK Ltd.
Pitfield, Milton Keynes, MK11 3LW, UK
UKHW022017190726
13853UKWH00005B/1973